'Did you h
date?'

'Yes, I had a   d
and vulnerable and very much alone tonight, and
she didn't want to stand in the hall and tell Will
that Mike Thomas had kissed her and it had been
a kiss devoid of any passion. At least on her part.

'Did he kiss you?'

Becky looked at him, wondering if he could read
her mind. 'That's none of your business.'

'You don't look like a woman who's been kissed.
Did he kiss you like this?' Will brushed his lips
against hers for a sweet, brief moment. Then Will
looked at her, and when she didn't answer, he
tried again. 'Or was it more like this?'

This time his arms went around her. This time her
hands crept up to his shoulders. She parted her
lips and he took her mouth with his tongue and
they kissed for long, heated moments.

He ended the kiss and smiled. '*Now* you look like
you've been kissed.'

KRISTINE ROLOFSON is also the author of
these novels in *Temptation*®

THE LAST MAN
IN MONTANA

BY

KRISTINE ROLOFSON

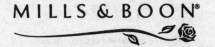

MILLS & BOON®

First published in Great Britain 1997 by Harlequin Mills & Boon Limited, Eton House, 18-24 Paradise Road, Richmond, Surrey TW9 1SR

© Kristine Rolofson 1997

ISBN 0 263 80525 5

21-9709

Printed and bound in Great Britain by Caledonian International Book Manufacturing Ltd, Glasgow

1

WILL CODY PARKED his rig on the west side of the gravel road and turned off the ignition. The dog beside him whined, so Will leaned over and opened the passenger door. The Australian shepherd jumped out and trotted over to the fence line. Lady was smart enough to keep away from traffic, not that there was any. The road was quiet, as empty as he remembered. And when he forced himself to look across the gravel toward the old homestead, a familiar knot tightened in his gut and his hands balled into fists.

It was a familiar reaction, and one that made him take a deep breath as he surveyed the metal sign hanging over the entrance. He planned to drive the two-mile road to the ranch house, but Will hesitated. He could get on the meanest bronco in Montana with less trepidation. But it was his mother's seventy-fourth birthday, his right knee ached like a bastard, and more than anything he wanted to take a couple of those fancy pain pills and sleep for twenty-four hours. He'd been driving all night and he hoped that when he did finally step out of the truck, he could straighten his leg and walk to the house without falling on his face.

His uncle would have rolled over in his grave at the thought of his "no-good nephew" inheriting thirty thousand acres of the best cattle land in the country, but J. W. McLean had left it all to him. It must have been a bitter pill for the old man to swallow, that he had no one else to leave the place to, only an elderly sister and a footloose rodeo rider. Will would have chuckled, if there was anything funny about returning to a place where he hadn't been welcome for sixteen years.

Still, nothing could harm him here. J.W. was dead and buried. One of the most detested men in Montana had died in his sleep, surprising those who'd said that old J.W. was "too mean to die." Well, his uncle had been mean, all right. The devil had better be watching his back.

Will whistled for the dog, shut the door after she hopped back in the cab and started up the truck. William Wyoming Cody was going home, whether he liked it or not. Not that it had ever been much of a home, but he'd learned one thing in sixteen years: a man didn't have to look back if he didn't want to.

"MAMA, THERE'S SOMEONE comin'," Pete announced. He was four years old and he liked to know things first, before anyone else.

Becky shaded her eyes with her hand and looked toward the road. Sure enough, a battered blue pickup hauling a small horse trailer was coming down the drive to the house. She went back to the plants, trying to find a few early tomatoes for the salad. Company at the ranch was nothing new these days. One of Maude's friends arriving early for the party wouldn't be unusual, though it would be anyone's guess why she'd be bringing her own horse. It was a big day here at the Silver Valley ranch, with the Not Dead Yet Club's first party starting in a couple of hours, along with the celebration for Maude's birthday. Maude wouldn't let anyone buy her presents, but had insisted on ordering three different kinds of birthday cake instead.

"Mama?" Pete tugged on her shirttail.

"What, honey?"

"I found another one."

Becky lifted her gaze from the tomato plants, swatted a fly from her arm and looked down at her son. He held a tiny black kitten in his arms. "I told you, Peter, those kittens are too young to be away from their mother. Go put it back where you found it, and be very careful."

"That makes six. I counted."

"Great. Go give it back to its mother."

"Okay." He didn't move. She found one more ripe tomato and put it in the bucket. That would have to do. Maude had told her not to bother making a green salad, but Becky wanted everything to be just right. She opened the gate, Peter following close behind, and stepped into the drive just as the visitor got out of the truck. He was tall, with a wide pair of shoulders, and a big black-and-white dog at his heels. He didn't look at all like someone Maude would hire, though, since he looked about forty years shy of seventy. And they weren't expecting the new horses until tomorrow.

"Hello," she called, walking toward him. "What can I do for you?"

His hat, looking as if it had seen as many miles as his truck, shaded his face. He wore typical work clothes: denim jeans and a plaid cotton shirt. The boots were scuffed, and he limped as he walked toward her. "Hello," he said, not smiling.

That face. She knew that face. She stared at the stranger who might not be a stranger at all.

He gave her an odd look. "I'm Will Cody and I'm looking for my mother. Is Maude around?"

Becky couldn't speak. It was as if the dry Montana wind had taken the words and blown them out of her head. She stood there, in her husband's faded jeans and

one of Maude's oldest shirts, perspiration thick on her
skin and cow manure stuck to her boots. She contem-
plated running like a crazy woman into the house, but
instead stayed rooted to the dirt and faced the one man
who threatened everything she'd worked for in the past
year. She opened her mouth to speak, but found she
couldn't say a word.

"You work here?" he asked, frowning a little.

She managed to nod, but he had already moved past
her on his way to the house, the dog following close behind.

"Good. Have someone take care of my horse," he said.

So Will Cody had returned. Without warning, and out
of the clear blue sky. He'd walked in and started giving
orders like he owned the place. Which he did. Which
could be a very big problem.

"Who was that, Mama?"

"Maude's son. Mr. Cody."

"Why's he here?"

"This is his ranch."

"It's Maude's ranch," Peter insisted.

She smiled down into his blue eyes. He was one smart
kid. "Yes, it's her home. Just like it's ours."

Peter thought about that for a moment. "Do I have to
put the kitty away?"

"Yes, you do." She glanced toward the house. Maude
would be thrilled. It wasn't every day that Will Cody
condescended to set foot on the Silver Valley ranch. They
should feel honored, blow trumpets, set off fireworks.
Feeling especially cowardly, Becky set the bucket of tomatoes by the fence. "I'll help you."

"What kind of dog was that? It had a lot of hair."

"I don't know. You'll have to ask Mr. Cody." Though
she hoped he wouldn't be here long enough to answer

questions. She'd see that his horse was stabled and fed, and she'd change her clothes and, if Tommy continued to sleep, finish the salad. She'd avoid the houseguest for as long as she could and maybe, with luck, he'd be gone before she'd have to see him again. Maybe he was here to see his mother, then leave. Maybe nothing would change.

Maybe.

Decker was out in front of the sagging bunkhouse, painting the trim white. He grinned when he saw them and waved toward his paint job. "Afternoon, Reb. How's it look?"

"Very nice," she told the old cowboy. His hands were so gnarled she didn't know how he held a paintbrush. "I think you were right to just paint the trim."

He dipped the brush into the bucket and with careful motions spread paint evenly on the board. "You know Maude. She wanted to paint the whole thing, but I like the gray just fine. Easier on the eyes."

"We have company."

He didn't stop painting. "I saw him."

"Is there anyone around who can take care of his horse?"

"A man usually takes care of his horse himself. Least that's the way it was in my day."

Becky chuckled. "You're welcome to tell him that yourself, Deck."

"He has a dog, too," Peter said.

"Nice kitten," the old man said, smiling at the boy. "He'll make a good mouser for the barn."

"Go put it back," Becky told Peter once again. "I'll wait for you here."

"'Kay," the child said, and the kitten woke up and started mewing.

She turned back to the elderly cowhand. "Do you think he's going to stay?"

Miles Decker shrugged. "No tellin' what that boy is up to. He hasn't been back since the day he turned eighteen. From what Maude says, he's not one to stay in one place too long. Which is a goldarn shame, too."

She didn't think it was a shame at all. She wanted him out of here before he could interfere. "He's limping."

That got the man's attention. "He's too old for rodeoin'. A man his age should know better."

Another elderly man stuck his head out the door. "You talkin' about me again?" He winked at Becky and shifted his hat off his forehead. "Decker here is a regular Mickleangelo, ain't he?"

The old cowboy was unperturbed. He moved to the other side of the doorway and kept on painting. "Willie's back," he said.

"Well, I'll be damned!" J. J. Malone's face creased into a wide grin. "It'll be good to have him around."

"He wants someone to take care of his horse," Miles muttered. "In my day—"

"A fellow looks after his own horse," a familiar voice said. The three turned around to see Will Cody standing behind them. A docile chestnut quarter horse stood beside him and tugged gently on the rope anchored to her halter.

"Well, I'll be," Miles said, putting down the brush. He shook Will's hand and, to Becky's surprise, looked as if he was trying to blink back tears. She'd never seen the old cowhand display much emotion, not even last winter when he'd had to put down his favorite horse. J.J. shook hands with him, too, and grinned like a kid at a circus.

"Guess you've come back," Miles said.

"Yeah. For a little while."

"Heard you got hurt."

"Yeah." Will looked embarrassed. "A bronc landed wrong. Messed up my knee."

"Too bad," J.J. said. "We heard you were heading for another championship season."

Will shook his head. "I'm sitting this one out. At least till I get this leg healed."

"Have you seen your mother yet?"

"No. I couldn't find her. I thought she might be out here."

"I'll tell her you're here," Becky offered, anxious to get away from him. She left the cowboys asking questions about the rodeo life as she headed to the barn. Men like Will Cody were all the same, full of themselves and full of stories that were only half-true. She had no patience for bullshit, not unless there was a real bull providing it.

She waved to Peter, who broke into a run when he rounded the corner of the barn, and waited for him to catch up to her.

"Come on, honey. I've got to get changed and check on Tommy. I'll race you back to the house!"

He grinned and took off, with Becky pretending that she couldn't keep up. She let him win, and they cleaned their boots together before entering the house through the back porch. She forgot all about the tomatoes until she entered the kitchen. Too late now. Becky looked at the clock over the stove. She had sixty minutes to get ready for company and tell Maude that her one and only son had finally come home.

"That's a fine woman," Miles Decker said, watching Will turn to look at the woman and her son.

"Yessir," J.J. agreed. "A fine woman."

Will watched her jog beside her son until they disappeared over near the old two-story house. So that was Becky McGregor, the woman his mother had hired to help with the housework. At first he hadn't known who she was. He hadn't been expecting such a young woman or someone so pretty, with yellow hair and big blue eyes. He'd guess she was hiding one hell of a body under those baggy clothes, too. A man could tell those things. "Mom told me she'd hired someone for the house."

"Oh, she don't just work in the house," J.J. said.

"What else does she do?"

The two old men looked at each other, then Miles kicked at a piece of dirt with the toe of his boot. "She earns her keep," he drawled. "She was widowed. Maude asked her to come here. She's been a big help to your ma."

Will looked around the cluster of old buildings. A couple of the sheds looked as if the next good wind would blow them down, and the bunkhouse didn't look much better. The fact that they were getting a new coat of paint seemed almost ridiculous. "So the bunkhouse is still standing after all this time. I thought you and Malone were over at the Circle Bar."

"We're back here now."

"I see that." So the old man didn't want to explain. Well, that was all right, he guessed. His uncle had had a knack for alienating people and everyone knew he'd been the meanest man in the county until the day he died.

"We take care of what we can," the old cowboy said, picking up the paintbrush again. "Your ma's fixing things up real nice."

"I'll be glad to take care of her for you," J.J. said, stepping over to run his hand along the mare's neck. "She's a beauty."

"I'd appreciate that," Will said, giving him the rope. He waited until J.J. left, then moved closer to the cowboy who had treated him like a son. "Is Maude all right?"

"Never better."

"That's a relief. She said her arthritis really bothered her last winter. Where's Hagman?"

"You'll have to ask Maude."

Will frowned. "He's the foreman. Don't you know where he is?"

"Ain't the foreman anymore. Maude fired him."

"Who's in charge now?"

"Well, you should talk to your ma about that. I'm helping."

Will surveyed the man, who must be at least eighty by now. He remembered following him around the ranch when he was old enough to walk. And Miles Decker had taught him how to ride and taught him how to land when he fell. He didn't want to hurt the man's feelings. He cleared his throat and tried a casual tone. "I thought you retired."

Miles met his gaze. "Maybe I would, if there was someone around who could run this place."

Like me. The message was clear. A Cody should be running the ranch. And maybe a Cody would have, if his uncle hadn't disowned him when he'd run off to join the rodeo. He'd just wanted a little freedom, a chance to be wild and show off and see the world. He'd wanted to prove he couldn't be bullied, that he had his pride. He hadn't known it would cost everything he cared about. "I didn't expect to own this place," he said. "I was disowned, remember?"

"Hell, Willie. That don't mean nothing no more, and you and I both know it."

Will wished he'd taken his pain pills when he'd been inside the house. He was tired of fighting the pain. He was tired of fighting a lot of things. "I don't know any such thing, Deck. I just came back to take care of business."

"Your ma will be glad. She said you would come."

"I should have been here before. She keeps telling me she's fine, not to worry. And I didn't, thinking Hagman was still here keeping things running for her."

"He and your uncle were two of a kind. Both ready to skin a neighbor to make a dollar."

Will's eyebrows rose. "I didn't know that."

The old cowboy met his gaze. "Well, I guess there's a lot of things you don't know."

Will nodded, which was the only thing he could do under the circumstances. He'd put every dime he had in the bank for years, waiting for the day when his mother would tell him she was ready to leave the ranch. She never complained, but he knew it was a hard life for a woman her age, and J.W. never spent a dollar on anything that would provide comfort. Chances are the roof still leaked and the pipes froze in the winter if you didn't leave the water running. He had more than enough to buy her a nice little condominium in Billings, in that new retirement community facing the Rockies. "I'm going to find her."

"You go ahead, son. You're one heck of a birthday present."

"MY SON?" Maude swiveled from the mirror. Her white hair was pulled back in a braid, a silver barrette holding it in place. She wore a white peasant dress with lavender embroidery and matching lavender cowboy boots. She didn't look seventy-four, but she was only five feet tall, with small bones, and people tended to underestimate her. "Willie is here?"

"Yep. You look great, by the way."

"Thank you, dear. He said he was coming for my birthday, but I didn't dare hope." She stood up and smoothed her skirt. "He's not going to like any of this," Maude said. "I love him dearly, but he's going to make trouble. I know it."

Becky hoped Maude was wrong. "Maybe not. Maybe he'll want to help."

"Help?" Maude squeaked. "You don't know him very well, do you?"

"I don't know him at all, Maude. I moved to town long after he left."

"Oh, that's right. Sometimes I forget..." She stopped, lost in thought for a few seconds. "It's been so long. I thought he'd never come back."

"Oh, he's back, all right. And he's looking for you."

"I'll be downstairs then." She looked at Rebecca's outfit and sighed. "Will you have time to get ready before the baby wakes?"

"I hope so."

"Where's Pete?"

"Oatey's feeding him, then I'll see if I can get him to rest for a while."

"Then you'd better hurry." She gave Rebecca a push toward the door. "Don't use your precious time worrying about my son."

"But the horses—"

"Are none of his business. He's not the type to put down roots, least of all here. Though I wish he would."

Becky couldn't think of anything to say to that. She wondered how she'd feel when Peter and Tommy Lee moved away from her and started their own lives. She'd be real happy to see them, no matter when they returned. Of course, if she lost this job she wasn't sure how she'd make it from now until they were grown. Becky hurried down the hall toward her room. The ranch house was enormous, built at the beginning of the century by a struggling family from Kentucky. Each generation had added on a wing or a porch, so the house sprawled in several directions. She and the kids had connecting rooms in the east wing, on the second floor, and it had taken Rebecca three weeks to find the shortcut down the kitchen staircase. The place was sparse, though, but she'd brought some of her own furniture to fill in a few empty places.

All things considered, she didn't have time to help Maude hostess her party. She should be at the barn, making sure everything was ready for tomorrow's delivery. There was fence to check in the east range, and Deck said he was worried about one of the cows in the Second Pasture. The cowboys had a name for every chunk of land on the thirty thousand acres.

She hurried into her room and, as quietly as possible so she wouldn't wake the sleeping child next door, undressed and showered. She changed into one of her few dresses, a Western-style blue cotton with a flouncy skirt. She'd bought it years ago for a dance, but it was still in style, at least for what Maude had in mind. The Not Dead Yet members were dressing up this Sunday afternoon, and Maude had insisted she attend. She wanted to help the older woman celebrate her birthday. Maude McLean Cody was someone special, and she owed her a lot. She'd do anything for the woman, including being nice to her son. Even if he didn't deserve to have such a wonderful mother.

THE KNEE WAS killing him. He could've kissed J.J. for offering to take care of the mare for him. And carrying on a conversation with Decker took more wits than he had available to use right now. He set his jaw and made his way to the long kitchen at the back of the house. He told Lady to wait outside, so the dog flopped on some grass underneath one of the trees. He'd hoped it would be empty, but a little kid was there eating a sandwich, and another elderly cowboy sat snoring with his head on the table.

Will looked around the room and half expected someone to kick him out. The room hadn't changed. It was still a farm kitchen, cluttered with cooking equipment, but his mother wasn't here baking bread and asking him how school had been. He took a deep breath, and the feeling of nausea subsided a little.

"Shh," the boy whispered, pointing to the cowboy. "He gets mad if you wake him up."

"Oatey has a temper," Will agreed, remembering the man from years ago. "What kind of sandwich is that?"

"Peanut butter and jelly."

Will moved over to the counter and eyed the contents of the platters spread out over the wooden surface. Covered in plastic wrap, it looked like enough food to feel all of Dry Gulch and then some. He lifted a corner of the plastic and took out a square piece of chocolate cake.

"You're gonna get in trouble," the kid said. "They don't like it if you sneak."

"Who doesn't?"

"Miss Maude and Mom."

"Well, don't tell them." He ate half the piece in one bite, then the other.

The boy glared at him. "They'll think I did it."

Will reached in and took another piece of cake. Chocolate with fudge frosting was his favorite, though he didn't know why women thought they had to put little frosting flowers on perfectly good food. He reached over and tried to hand it to the boy, but the stubborn kid just looked at him. "Don't you want a piece?"

"Well, yeah, but—"

"Take it," Will urged, stepping closer. He set it on the boy's plate. "I'll tell them I took two pieces. They can't do anything to me."

"Your mother will."

"Nope. It doesn't work that way when you're grown-up."

The boy glanced over at the sleeping cowboy before he reached for the cake. "It doesn't?"

"No." Will limped over to the refrigerator and surveyed the food inside. "Looks like they're getting ready for a party."

"Yeah." Pete licked his fingers. "The ladies are coming."

"What ladies?" His mother had never been one for socializing.

"I dunno. Just the ladies."

Will took out a plate full of roast beef and set it on the counter, then found the mustard behind two bowls of Jell-O. "Want some Jell-O?"

"Nope. It dents," the boy answered.

"Yeah. Better to leave the Jell-O alone, all right."

"You'd better be quiet." He pointed to the cowboy whose snoring had stopped. "I'll hafta take a nap when he wakes up."

Will quickly slapped a sandwich together with bread from the loaf he'd found on top of the refrigerator. "A nap? Aren't you a little old for naps?"

The boy nodded glumly. "Ma doesn't think so."

"What's your name?"

"Peter McGregor. I know who you are."

"Yeah?"

"Miss Maude has your pictures in her room."

Will found a container of punch when he put the meat away, so he got a glass and sat down at the table to eat his sandwich. His knee throbbed harder. After he ate he'd take another couple of pills, wish his mother a happy birthday and spend the rest of the day letting Maude fuss over him. He eyed the boy who was watching him pour himself a drink. "What's the matter?"

"You're not supposed to get into the punch."

Will took a long swallow of the fruity drink, popped a couple of pain pills, then drained the rest of the glass. "I told you, grown-ups can do whatever they want." He refilled his glass to prove the point. The kid was starting to get on his nerves, so he tried to ignore him.

Which wasn't going to be easy, especially since the little boy wouldn't stop staring at him. Will tried to pretend he didn't notice and looked at Oatey instead. His uncle had fired Oatey for sleeping through his shift. Of course, he hadn't waited to find out that the cowhand had been up for two nights in a row nursing a couple of sick calves.

He didn't know how his mother had stood living with her brother all those years. He'd bet there weren't three people in town who hadn't been screwed by old J. W. McLean.

Oatey opened his eyes and blinked. Then blinked again as he focused on Will's face. "Well, I'll be," he said, rubbing his eyes. "Haven't seen you in more 'n twenty years, son. How've you been?"

Will hid a smile. He tried to guess what the man's age would be now. Seventy? Eighty? Hard to tell. "Fine, Oatey. How about you?"

The old man shrugged. "Good days and bad days, just like everyone else. Don't know what I would've done if your ma hadn't asked me back."

"She's hired back a lot of cowhands?" What was going on around here? He'd have to talk to his mother about business. Tomorrow.

"I 'spect so. Now that J.W.'s gone, the men came back when Miss Maude asked them to." He nodded toward the boy. "You met my pal Petey?"

"Yeah, sure did."

Oatey stood up and stretched. "He's gotta take a nap now, and I think I'll take one, too."

"You just did," the boy said.

"Yeah, well, I was warmin' up for the real thing."

"Will says I'm too old for naps," the boy announced.

"Yeah?" Oatey didn't look impressed. "Well, we'll ask your ma what she thinks. She's the boss around here, ain't she?"

Peter shot Will a disgusted look. "Yeah, she's the boss."

"Sorry, kid," he said. "Guess you'd better go with Oatey."

"See ya later," the boy said. "Hope you don't get caught."

Will kept a straight face. "Thanks."

"He never gets caught," Maude said. Will looked over to see his mother standing in the doorway. She moved out of the way so Oatey could take the boy upstairs. "See you later, Peter. We'll save you some cake."

The boy turned and looked at Will, who winked at him.

"William," his mother said, and Will started to stand up.

"Don't get up," Maude said. "Finish your lunch. It's good to see you sitting at the table again."

She bent over and gave him a kiss on the cheek. "I knew you wouldn't forget my birthday, but why didn't you tell me you were coming?"

"I wasn't sure myself." He winced as he moved his leg over so she could sit down in the chair near him. "Happy birthday," he said, pulling a small box from his shirt pocket.

"You're hurt again, and you shouldn't be buying me presents. You do too much as it is."

"Open it," he said, and Maude lifted the lid to reveal a pair of intricately carved silver earrings.

"They're beautiful," she said, kissing him on the cheek. "Thank you, dear." She frowned at his leg. "What happened?"

"Just a little problem with the knee."

"When are you going to stop this? You're too old to compete with those youngsters."

He grinned at her and poured some more punch into his glass. "Beats settling down, I guess. And the money is good."

"Can you stay the night?"

"I'll stay a few days, Mother. To sort out things here. We'll need to talk. And why haven't you sent the accounts to me?"

She looked confused. "I didn't send them?"

"No."

"Oh. I *thought* I did." She patted his hand. "Now don't even think about that. You don't have to worry about me or those complicated ledgers, either. Not anymore."

"Why's that?" He was starting to feel pretty relaxed. Maybe coming back to Silver Valley hadn't been such a bad idea after all. That eerie feeling had passed, and now he began to feel ridiculous for stalling for so many months.

"Let's talk about it tomorrow. I'm a little busy right now, dear."

"All right." He could be agreeable when he wanted to be. "When's the party?"

"Any minute. I want you to meet my friends. They've all heard about you and seen my scrapbook."

"You look good, Mother. You feeling okay?"

"Never better." She patted his hand and stood up. "Come help me greet my guests as soon as you're through here."

"Maybe I should clean up first."

"Don't bother." She smiled. "The ladies will love that scruffy cowboy look you have."

He fingered his two-day growth of beard. "You sure?"

"Positive, Willie. Maybe before lunch you could tell us a little bit about the rodeo. The ladies would love that. No one knew we were going to have a guest speaker at our first meeting."

"I'm not much of a speaker," Will protested. "First meeting of what?"

But his mother didn't answer. She was already out the door in a whirl of white ruffles and silver jewelry. Will blinked and leaned back in his chair, then poured himself another glass of that punch. He didn't know what was in it, but it was the tastiest fruit juice he'd had in a long time.

He gingerly propped his foot on an empty chair and began to smile. Thank the Lord for small favors. His knee was finally starting to numb up, and the ghost of J. W. McLean was nowhere to be seen.

2

"MAUDE? IS THERE, uh, something the matter with him?" Becky asked her employer. She didn't want to be rude and suggest that Maude's son might be falling-down drunk, but on the other hand she didn't want anything to spoil Maude's birthday party. The woman had worked too hard to have her special day ruined.

"Well, I don't know," Maude said. She and Becky stood together in a corner of the large living room and watched as Will answered questions from several gray-haired ladies. There was a silly grin on his face, and from what Becky could hear he was slurring some of his words.

"I mean, is he always so . . . social?" Becky hoped she was being polite. Maybe Maude was used to her son's drinking and didn't think anything of it. That was all they needed now, for a drunk to have inherited the Silver Valley.

"I think he's drunk," his mother declared. "He was hitting the punch pretty hard out in the kitchen."

"The *rum* punch? I didn't think I made it that strong."

"Maybe if you drink enough of it, that's what happens." She looked around at her guests to see if anyone else was getting tipsy. "Do you think it's affecting everyone?"

"No," Becky said. "Just him. But just in case, maybe you'd better start the program so people can eat."

Maude smiled up at her. "Good idea, my dear. You're always so full of good ideas."

Becky wished that were true. "What do you want me to do to help?"

"Nothing for now. Just keep an eye on my boy," Maude said. "If he starts to fall over, try to stop him from crashing into any of the food."

Great. This was her day off, and instead of enjoying Maude's party or working in the barn, she was stuck baby-sitting a has-been rodeo champion who couldn't hold his liquor and was most likely going to throw a fit when he found out who was running the ranch. She edged closer to the group of women around the cowboy and listened to the conversation.

"The worst horse I ever rode?" He rubbed his jaw as if he was thinking real hard. It was a little overdone, Becky figured, but the women didn't seem to mind. "Well, I guess that would be a little bas— 'Scuse me, ladies." He smiled, and one of the women giggled. "I haven't been in the comp'ny of ladies for a long time."

She would just bet he hadn't. She edged closer as he swayed to the left, then regained his balance.

"Now, where was I?" The chin thing again. Now *that* was getting annoying. "That would have to be in Texas, at a rodeo over in Fort Worth. A horse called Texas Tony that no one knew anything about." He chuckled. "I was on him for about three seconds, then—splat—flat on my back and the goddamn horse came back and tried to stomp on me." He widened his eyes. "Took four clowns to get him away. Can you b'lieve that?"

No, Becky thought. She couldn't. "Are you sure it wasn't a bull?" she asked. "I mean, this sounds like a bull story to me."

He shook his head, as serious as he could be while drifting to the left again. She reached out and grabbed his arm before he crashed into Maude's new lamp. "No, ma'am." He narrowed his eyes and tried to focus on her face. "Honey, have we met?"

"No."

"In Vegas. At the finals."

"No. Maybe you'd better sit down before you fall down, cowboy."

"I'm fine." He gave her another silly grin. "I'd be better if you came a little closer."

"How many bulls do you think you've ridden?" someone asked.

"I dunno. Can't count. About a hundred stock a year, I guess. Broncs and bulls, makes no diff'rence."

"Don't you ever get hurt?"

"All the time, ma'am. I got myself a bad knee now, but it ain't hurtin' me too much right at the moment."

One of the women smiled at her. "You'd better get some coffee in him, Becky. My Chester used to get like that sometimes."

"Thanks, Mrs. Arnold. I'll do my best."

"We'd better get something to eat," Mrs. Arnold told the others. "I think that Maude just set out lunch." The ladies moved toward the buffet table.

"I think I know you," Will muttered. "Bobbie? How the hell have you been?" He put an arm around her shoulder and pulled her against his side.

"I'm not—"

"Colored your hair, too." He sniffed. "I like that perfume, too. You wear that jest fer me, little lady?"

Becky tried to pull away without making a scene, but the cowboy's arm was an iron band holding her close. "I'm not Bobbie," she said, keeping her voice as low as she could. "And don't try to pull that 'little lady' crap on me."

"Ladies!" Maude banged her glass with a spoon and the conversation stopped as all eyes turned to their hostess. Maude stood in front of the stone fireplace and smiled at her guests. "Thank you all for coming today. We're planning a few special events this summer, so I want you to dust off your saddles and grab your boots, because the Not Dead Yet Club ladies are going to quit knitting and start riding."

"Dead what?" Will said, a little too loud.

"Shh," Becky told him. "Shut up for a minute."

Maude ignored her son. "Is everyone here?"

"'Cept Millie Freeman," someone called out. "Her daughter-in-law took sick, so she's home with the grandchildren."

"I hope it's not serious," Maude said.

"Nah," said Millie's neighbor. "She'll be here next week for the ride."

Will belched, and several women stared at him, including his mother. "What ride?"

"Never mind," Becky told him. She moved to the side, hoping he'd follow. "How about you and me going to find something to drink?" She hoped that would get him out of the living room and away from the women. It wasn't any of his business what his mother chose to do with her spare time, especially since he hadn't set foot on the Silver Valley ranch since the day he turned eighteen. At least, that was the story that Decker told.

"Well, now you're talkin'," he said, an idiot grin plastered on his face. He was incredibly handsome, better-looking than that picture in *American Horseman* magazine that Maude had stuck to the side of her mirror.

"What ever happened to that twin sister of yours? She still racing barrels, too?"

"She got married," Becky lied. "Has triplets now and gained two hundred pounds. You want to see her?"

Will gulped. "Triplets?"

"Yep." Becky edged closer to the doorway, and the cowboy tried to go with her, but his legs didn't seem to want to move too well. "Hey, can't you walk?"

He looked down at his booted feet. "I used to know how," he said, and looked at her with a confused expression on his face. "Damn knee."

"I don't think your knee's the problem."

"No?"

"You've had too much to drink, pal."

He shook his head. "Can't drink. Not now."

"You need to lie down," she told him. "Don't you think that's a good idea?"

He stared at her, then he broke into a grin. "Hell, honey, I haven't been to bed in a hell of a long time. If you know what I mean."

"Becky?" Maude called. "Do you need help?"

"I got him," she assured her boss.

Maude turned back to the ladies. "It seems my son has had too much punch and not enough sleep. He drove all night to be home for my birthday," she announced proudly.

The ladies turned toward William and applauded. He tried to bow, but lurched against a leather chair.

"Come on, cowboy. Let's get you bedded down for the night."

"Yes, ma'am."

Maude raised her glass. "I'm going to ask you to drink a toast to my brother." She waited while the ladies refilled their glasses. There was a slight murmur that ran through the group, but Maude waited patiently. "As you all know, my older brother wasn't the most loved man in Montana."

"I'll drink to that!" somebody called, and several ladies giggled.

Will stopped struggling and turned to look at his mother. "What the hell is she talking about?"

"Let's go." Becky tried to leave, tugging on Will's waist without much success. It was like trying to move a tree.

"Nope," he said, then lifted his glass toward his mother. "What're we drinking to, Ma?"

"To a new era on the old SV," she answered, raising her voice and her glass. "My brother did a lot of rotten things in his day. Some people would say 'what's done is done' but, as you all know, I don't believe that."

The audience was mesmerized. Becky once again tried to move the cowboy toward the door, but his arm tightened around her and held her still. "Quit struggling, darlin'."

"So here's to making things right," Maude said. "And here's to a summer full of adventure!"

Becky managed to move Will as the ladies lifted their glasses and drank to an exciting future. She got him as far as the door, then his arms lost their grip around her and he slid slowly to the floor and passed out.

She looked back to see if anyone had noticed, but luckily he'd fallen forward into the empty dining room. His boots were in the living room, but none of the ladies would notice unless they tripped over his feet. She could drag him that far, if she had to, but he was heavier than she thought. And a deadweight.

She checked to make sure he was breathing, then hurried upstairs to find Oatey, but the old cowhand was sound asleep on the floor by the crib. Peter was sitting in bed playing with his action figures.

"Can I get up now?"

She kept her voice low, but the baby stirred. "Not yet." She knelt by Oatey and gently shook his shoulder. "Oatey?"

He opened his eyes and blinked at her. "Yes, ma'am?"

"I need your help for a minute. Sorry to wake you."

"I wasn't sleepin'. Just closin' my eyes for a sec, that's all."

Becky tried not to smile. "Can you come downstairs with me?"

"Yes, ma'am." He sat up slowly, then managed to stand up by hanging on to the crib. The baby sat up and smiled at them.

"Hi, Tommy," Becky said.

"Get up now," he said, raising his hands.

"In a minute. You stay here with Peter. Mommy will be back in a minute."

The toddler looked over at his brother and grinned. "Hi."

"Hi, Tommy."

"I'll be right back," she told the boys. As soon as she and Oatey were out the door, she tried to explain what had happened but Oatey didn't seem to understand what she was talking about. Once they stood in the dining room—a useless room that was too cold in the winter and impractical in the summer—and stared down at Maude's son, Oatey scratched his head.

"Never knew a ladies' fruit punch would do that to a fella," he said.

Peter tugged on his mother's skirt. "Must be those pills he took. They looked kinda big."

"Pills?" She looked down at her son. "You're supposed to be upstairs. Go. Now." Peter sighed and started toward the stairs.

"For his leg, I'll bet," Oatey said. "He looked like it was hurtin' him pretty bad."

So the idiot cowboy had combined pills and alcohol and passed out. She wondered if she should get him to the hospital. "Do you think he could die?"

Oatey bent down and rolled Will onto his back, then he put his ear down to Will's chest. "Heart sounds strong." He reached into Will's shirt pocket and pulled out a plastic vial. "Guess this here's the culprit," he said, handing the bottle to Becky. She read it, but the medication didn't mean anything.

"Let's get him in a bed somewhere until I can call a doctor."

Oatey obligingly picked up Will's arms. "Where do you want him?"

"The den, I guess. There's no way we're going to get him upstairs."

Will groaned when Becky moved his feet.

"He's alive," Oatey announced. "I think we oughta let him sleep it off."

"I don't want him to die," Becky said. "Maude wouldn't like that."

"No, ma'am, but this boy is stronger than an ox. He ain't gonna die. Not now, not when he's finally back home."

They managed to get him through the dining room, around the chairs and out to the hall. Then they rested before heading into the other wing where the offices were. They got him settled on a braided rug, rolled him on his side and tucked a pillow under his head.

"Now what?"

"He shouldn't be alone."

"I'll stay with him," Oatey said, panting as he sat down on the couch. "You go get the little boys and bring 'em back here. No reason why they can't play down here and I'll watch all three."

Becky hurried back to the living room and found Maude. She took her aside and whispered, "Your son passed out. He took some pain pills with his lunch. And then started drinking that rum punch. Do you think we should call a doctor?"

Maude shook her head. "Theresa's here. She's retired, but she might know what we should do." She hurried off and returned with a tall, big-boned woman who looked as if she didn't panic easily.

"Dr. Ames," she said, shaking Becky's hand. "Don't think we've met."

"No, but—"

"Where is he?"

Theresa Ames followed them down the hall and into the den where the cowboy lay sleeping. She looked at the pills, questioned everyone as to the amount of alcohol in the punch and how much they'd seen Will drink, then nodded. "Let him sleep it off. These pills are strong and shouldn't be combined with alcohol, but there wasn't much in that punch. You said he was driving all night?"

"Yes."

"I'd let him sleep. He's not unconscious."

"If you're sure," Maude said, looking concerned.

"I'll call the hospital and double-check," Theresa assured her. "If they think there's a reason to treat him, we'll bring him in."

A look of relief crossed Maude's face. "Thank you, Theresa. I appreciate it."

"No problem." The doctor turned to Oatey. "See if you can get his boots off and find him a bed. Maude said he has an injured knee." Becky and the old cowboy nodded. "Leave his pants on, then. Wouldn't want to make that leg worse."

Since the thought of undressing Will Cody hadn't entered Becky's mind, she agreed right away. "No, of course not."

"Come on, Maude," the elderly doctor said. "Let's go eat lunch and plan that pack trip. When are the horses coming in?"

"Tomorrow," Maude said, looking at her son. "Did he say how long he was staying, Becky?"

"No."

"I hope he's not going to be difficult," the older woman said.

Oatey guffawed. "Doesn't look 'difficult' right now, does he?"

The three women agreed, and Becky went upstairs to retrieve her children. She had more to worry about than whether or not Will Cody could get his boots off.

MAUDE WISHED HE'D wake up. Oatey and some of the boys had managed to get him into a bed in one of the spare rooms, so he was tucked under the covers and sleeping soundly. That dog of his had cried at the back-door until Oatey had let her in and showed her where Will slept. She lay down on the rug, her head on her paws, and looked about as sad as a dog could get. Maude sat on the faded corduroy sofa and watched her son.

It was evening before her guests left, with sunset highlighting the sky with a beautiful array of colors. She'd seen everyone off, waved goodbye, promised to show them the horses next week. It was going to be a good summer. Her brother had been gone almost a year now. He hadn't been an easy man to love, but she'd done her best. Even after he'd driven Will off the place, she'd tried in vain to mend the fences. Now he was gone and Will was back for the first time in many years.

Oh, she'd flown to different cities to see her son. He'd bought that little place in Billings and they'd spent some nice holidays together. She'd hoped he would settle down with some nice gal and have kids. She would have liked Christmases with grandchildren to spoil. But that's what happened when you had your first and only child at forty-one. There was a good chance you wouldn't live long enough to see who your grandchildren took after.

"Maude?"

She looked up to see Miles Decker standing in the doorway. He'd been one of her husband's best friends; Jack used to say there wasn't a better man in all of Montana. "Hi, Miles. Come on in."

He glanced toward the bed. "Well, I don't want to wake him."

"I don't think there's any chance of that." She patted the empty space beside her. "Come sit with me a minute."

Miles stepped carefully over the dog. "That his?"

The dog wagged her tail and looked at the old cowboy. "I guess so. I heard he brought his horse, too."

"Maybe that means he's staying."

"Or he's on his way somewhere else," Maude reminded her old friend. "He hasn't stepped foot on this ranch for sixteen years."

Miles cleared his throat. "About time he came back, then."

"You think he's come back for good?"

"It's hard to tell, Maudie. He's been gone a long time without putting down roots. Maybe he's decided to settle down and run this place for you."

Maude sighed. "I'd like that. I know there's more we could do to make ends meet. Becky does what she can, and does a good job, too, but we're going to be busy with the horses and our guests." She turned to look at her old friend. "I hope Will understands and doesn't change anything."

"You might not have a choice, Maudie. Considering J.W.'s will and all."

"I know. It's just going to be . . . awkward if he doesn't approve."

"Mebbee he will," Decker said. "Mebbee he'll like the idea of putting down roots and working with a beautiful young woman."

"Do you think Will and Becky will like each other?"

Miles sighed. "I dunno. I'm not much for matchmaking. Hell, Maude, I never even got married, haven't had a date in thirty years."

The two were quiet as they studied the young man in the bed. "He's a handsome devil," his mother said with a sigh. "I don't think Becky would be impressed by a handsome face, though."

"Nope."

"And he's never been around children. But I'll bet he'd make a good father, given half a chance."

Miles looked doubtful, but he nodded. "Anyone with half a heart would like those kids of hers. Don't give no one any trouble, those kids don't."

"True. They're quite lovable. And our Becky's a pretty girl, with a good disposition."

"Hardheaded, though."

Maude sighed. "That's true, but we can always hope."

Miles nodded, and reached down to pet the dog. "Yep. Hopin' don't cost nothin'."

"WHO WAS THAT man, Mama?"

"I told you, Peter. Miss Maude's son, remember?" She fixed him a plate of leftovers from the party. The ladies hadn't eaten as much as she and Maude had figured they would, which meant they wouldn't have to cook tomorrow.

"He took some cake without asking," Peter whispered, leaning closer.

"That's okay. I guess he can take whatever he wants."

"That's what he said. I wanna get big like that, so I can eat cake all the time. With my fingers."

Becky smiled. "Well, that's one of the advantages, I guess." Why had Maude's son decided to come home after all these years? Maude would be thinking he was going to stay and run the ranch now that it was his. Becky didn't think so. Men who liked to rodeo didn't change. Maude would get her hopes up and then he'd head out again, disappointing everyone. They needed help around here. The ranch was just too much to run among the six of them, and it was about time they all faced facts.

But was an injured rodeo king the answer? She wished she knew.

Becky poured herself a glass of the rum punch and leaned against the kitchen counter. The cowboys all did their best, and gave her good advice, too. But there was the haying to do and machinery to repair. The horses were coming and would need to be settled in. Maude had paid top money to buy the best, but it would be Becky's job to make sure they were well taken care of.

She didn't know how many more things she could take care of. And maybe Will would decide she didn't have to take care of any of it. He'd fire her, or send her back to the kitchen. He'd hire someone like Hagman who wouldn't understand that the ranch hands couldn't work twelve-hour shifts anymore.

SHE FELT MORE CHEERFUL the next morning. Becky poured herself a cup of coffee and took it over to the table. The kitchen was dark, the shades pulled against the bright summer sun. She'd been up for four hours, since six, and the heat was starting to get to her. July in Montana could be excruciating. By noon she'd be ready to come indoors and play with the children, but for now she'd have to get back outside and make sure the stalls were ready. Deck had put up a new fence in the horse corral and the three other men had spent last week cleaning the barn. It was slow work, but it had gotten done in time. The trick was to give the men plenty of notice when she wanted something done.

The house was quiet, with the boys "helping" in the barn and Maude gone to town. The rodeo rider was most likely still sleeping it off, thank goodness. The less she had to deal with him the better she'd be.

She didn't know what she was so afraid of. It was Will's ranch now, Will's business to decide how things should be run. His mother would say nothing was going to change, but Becky had a gut feeling that life could be very different from here on if she wasn't careful. She would stay out of the fancy cowboy's way as best she could.

Until he walked into the kitchen. He was showered and shaved and in clean clothes, and he looked very handsome. He ran his hand through damp, dark hair and smiled at her. "'Mornin'."

"'Morning," she said, taking a sip of coffee. She watched as he found the mugs easily enough and poured himself a cup of coffee. He was still limping, but not as badly as yesterday. Maybe sleeping for over eighteen hours had helped him after all.

He leaned against the counter, drank half the coffee then refilled his mug before coming over to the table and sitting across from her. "Did we meet yesterday?"

"Not exactly. You thought I was someone else."

"I did? Who?"

"Never mind. I'm Becky McGregor."

"Will Cody." He held out his hand and she shook it, feeling a bit silly. He looked harmless this morning. She took her hand back and wrapped it around her coffee cup.

"What did I do yesterday? All I remember is being around a lot of women." He gave her a sheepish look. "Then everything went blank."

"You passed out."

"I did?"

"Didn't anyone ever tell you that pills and alcohol are a pretty lethal combination?"

He stared at her for a minute, then realization dawned. "The fruit punch. No wonder it tasted so good."

"You didn't know there was rum in it?"

Will shook his head. "I was thirsty. It was in the fridge. Your kid told me it was for the party, but I drank it anyway."

Becky took another swallow of coffee. "It caught up with you. You were entertaining the ladies for a while, until you fell over. We had a doctor look at you, but she said you weren't going to die."

"*She* said?"

"One of your mother's friends."

"Oh."

They sat in silence for a few awkward minutes. Becky finished her coffee and made a move to leave the kitchen. "Guess I'd better get back to work."

"What do you do here?"

"Anything that Maude wants me to." Becky reached for her hat, but Will stopped her.

"Is she well?"

"Sure."

He didn't look as if he believed her. "I think she's too old for this kind of life. I'm thinking of taking her to Billings with me."

Becky stared at him for a long moment before she could speak. "I think you'd better ask her," she managed to say. "She seems pretty happy."

Will shook his head. "She can't run this place all alone."

"She's not," Becky said. "She has help."

"Not enough. Not the right kind. Besides, she ought to be enjoying her sunset years."

"Her what?"

"Sunset years. I found her a place near me. She won't have to lift a finger to do a thing. Everything's done for her, even her meals."

Becky put her mug in the sink, her hat on her head, and headed for the door. Before she left the kitchen she stopped and looked at the man sitting at the table. "You know what I think?" He frowned, obviously not liking her tone. "*I* think you've fallen on your head too many times." With that she turned around and stomped through the back porch.

He caught up with her at the horse corral, as she was listening to J.J. report on the sick cow, and Cal waited his turn to talk to her about the schedule.

"Better, I reckon," J.J. said, swatting a fly away from his face. "Calf's doin' fine now, too. You decided about hayin' yet?"

"Next week, I think. We'll take turns driving."

The old man nodded, then grinned at Will. "Hey, boy. Heard you slept real good last night."

"Guess there're no secrets around here."

Malone chuckled. "Oh, I reckon there's a few left. You looking for Maude?"

"Where is she?"

Becky answered for him. "In town. She said she had errands to do this morning."

"She goes alone?"

She ignored his disapproving look. "When she wants to."

"What happened to Rob Hagman?"

Becky turned to face the tall cowboy. She hated having to look up, but there was no help for it. "He was let go."

"Why?"

"He was having trouble working for Maude. He acted like it was the other way around. Maude fired him."

"My mother wouldn't—" He stopped and stared down at her. "And who's in charge now?"

There was no getting around it. She put her hands on her hips and glared back at him. "Me."

"You." He shook his head as if he didn't believe her. "Who the hell are you?"

"The foreman of this ranch, Mr. Cody."

His eyes narrowed. "Since when?"

"Since Maude hired me."

J.J. cleared his throat. "Car comin'," he said. "Most likely Maude. You two want to take this somewheres else? I got work to do."

"What the hell is going on around here?" Will Cody folded his arms across his chest and waited for Becky to give him an answer.

"The foreman is gone," Becky said. "Every hand on this place is over seventy. I was hired to cook, but instead I'm trying to run this ranch for your mother because her *son* can't be bothered to come back here and take over."

"My uncle wouldn't let me set foot on this place."

"He's been dead for nine months."

"And I've been working," Will said. "Not that it's any of your business."

"Well, we're all glad you're a big-time rodeo hero, but we've got work to do." With that, Becky jammed her hat on her head and went into the barn. Let Mr. Will Wyoming Big-Belt-Buckle Cody chew on that for a while.

3

LORD, HIS HEAD ACHED. He didn't want to stand there by the corral looking like an idiot, but he didn't seem to have much choice. He was going to look like an idiot no matter where he stood, he guessed. Becky McGregor had that effect on him.

The woman was a yellow-haired hellion. He didn't know what on earth his mother was doing hiring someone with such a nasty temper, but then again, Will thought, looking around at the rest of the ranch staff, Maude had collected the oddest assortment of ranch hands ever to gather in Montana. None of them under seventy, except for the woman.

And a woman, especially so young and inexperienced, had no business running a ranch the size of the Silver Valley. He would tell his mother what he thought as soon as possible. When his head cleared, he was going to have quite a meeting with his mother and plan her future. She was too old for ranch life, and it was about time she realized that. The ranch and she had had their day, and it was time to quit.

He turned to J.J. "Where's Deck this morning?"

"Working another shift." The old man coughed.

"Doing what?"

J.J. spit in the dirt. "I guess you could say we're busy with the little guys," he drawled. "Your ma's waving at you."

Will would have liked to ask about what exactly the calves needed, but he turned to see his mother walking carefully toward him. She looked more fragile than ever, her seventy-four years were starting to show. Still, there was a twinkle in her eyes. It was time, long past time, for her to retire. He couldn't wait to tell her what he had planned.

"Will!" she called. "You're awake!"

When she came closer she hugged him, wrapping her arms around his waist. She felt frail, as if she might break apart at any minute. "I hope I didn't ruin your party. I guess I passed out."

She backed up a step to look up at him. "The ladies thought you were charming, at least most of the time. I'm just glad you're all right. How's the knee?"

"Better. I guess it was good that I got off it for as long as I did."

"Good. I wish you'd quit that kind of life," his mother said. "Have you ever thought about what you'll do when you can't compete anymore?"

She'd given him the perfect opening. "I have a few ideas. In fact," he said, taking her arm, "let's go into the house and talk about it."

Her face lit up. "Really, Will? You know how much I'd always hoped that you'd come home," she said. "I knew it was impossible when J.W. was alive, but I never gave up hope."

"That's not exactly—"

"I know, I know. You liked rodeoing, too. And I can't blame you, not when you were making all that money. Ranching's a hard life, and I didn't expect—"

"Mother," he tried, before she really got going. "That's not what I'm talking about."

"It's not?"

J.J. cleared his throat. "Truck's comin'."

Maude and Will looked toward the road. It was something big, Will saw. Trailing dust and going slowly.

"Where's Becky? Is she ready?"

The cowardly hellion hadn't come out of the barn again. "Ready for what?"

Maude beamed. "Today's the big day. Hasn't anyone told you?"

"Nope. No one around here wants to tell me anything." He really should have taken some aspirin. He pulled his hat down to shade his eyes and waited for his mother to explain.

"The horses are coming."

"What horses?"

"The horses I purchased last month."

"You shouldn't be buying horses," he said, staring down at her. "What kind of horses?"

Becky came out of the barn and Maude waved her over. "Come tell Will about the horses, Becky. I keep forgetting what kind they are."

His eyes narrowed as the young woman came closer, but he ignored her and looked down at his mother. "You bought a special breed? Why on earth would you do that?"

"They're called Peruvian Pasos," Becky explained, standing next to Maude. "Your mother saw them at a stock show last spring."

Will turned to her. "Excuse me, miss, but I'm asking my mother the questions."

"Will!" Maude frowned at him. "Becky can answer any questions she wants to. She's my foreman now."

"I heard." *Temporary* foreman.

"Then don't be rude."

"Don't make me be," he countered. "How in the hell can a ranch this size be run by someone so young?"

Maude looked like she wanted to take him over her knee, the way she used to when he did something wrong. "We're doing just fine, thank you very much."

"We'll see," he said, looking at Becky. "How long have you been here, anyway?"

"About a year and a half."

"And how long have you been acting as foreman?"

"Since Hagman quit, about six months ago."

"And in six months you've started a horse-breeding operation and—" Will stopped before he pointed out that eighty-year-old cowboys shouldn't be solely responsible for all the work. J.J. was still standing there watching him, and he didn't want to insult the old man.

"And what?"

Maude tugged on Becky's arm. "Here they come."

"Later," he said, taking a step back that twisted his knee. "I'll talk to you later." He tried to sound like he was in charge, but neither woman was paying any attention to him. They were staring down the road like it was Christmas morning and Santa was coming. His mother even looked like she wanted to jump up and down, which she couldn't, of course, with the arthritis and all. She sure was excited about the horses. Peruvian Pasos? He'd never heard of them. He hoped like hell they weren't those miniature horses that Easterners seemed so crazy about. He wouldn't let them unload the damn things if that was the case.

He walked over and leaned against the corral next to J.J. "You have any idea what's going on here, Malone?"

"Well, Miss Maude is sure excited about these horses. They're s'posed to really be something."

"Never heard of them."

"Me neither, Willie. But then again, I don't get out much."

Will hid a smile and watched as two horse trailers drove past the house and headed toward them. Maude waved at the driver of the first truck, and when he'd come to a stop near the barn, walked over to greet him. He'd never seen his mother so excited about a horse. As far as he knew she hadn't ridden in years. This had to be Becky McGregor's idea. He'd bet his own mare on it.

He watched while the horses were unloaded, Becky looking each one over carefully and then setting them loose in the paddock. His mother had bought five mares and a stallion, and she and Becky were clucking over them like they were babies. And the horses stood there like babies, too, as if they weren't sure what to do.

"Pretty, ain't they?" Malone said.

All six were a rich chestnut color, with full manes and tails, though set lower than typical quarter horses. They were good-size horses, with a gentle look about them. "I guess," Will said, walking with the cowboy to see the horses.

Maude signed some papers, handed the first driver a white envelope and offered the men something cold to drink. The first man shook his head, and within minutes they were on their way, dust trailing from the tires.

"Well?" Maude said, coming to stand beside her son at the fence. "What do you think of my new babies?"

"What are they again?"

"Peruvian Pasos," she said.

"Supposed to be the smoothest-riding horse in the world." Becky perched on the fence rail. "They're from South America, descended from Spanish war-horses."

"Do either of you want to tell me why we need Spanish war-horses in Montana?"

"For riding, of course," his mother said. "They're for people with arthritis or bad backs or any kind of injury that makes it difficult to ride. I want to ride again," she declared.

"But—"

"No two hooves hit the ground at the same time," Becky interjected. "That's why they're so comfortable to ride. It's a gait called *paso llano*, which means 'fast walk.'"

I'd like to fast walk those fancy horses right off the Silver Valley ranch, Will thought. His mother had no business thinking she was going to start riding again at the age of seventy-four. She was moving to Billings to take it easy. "And do either of you know how to train them?" He couldn't keep the sarcasm from his voice.

"They're already trained," Becky said. "We bought them ready to ride."

"I think we should try them out," Maude said. "Which one do you want, Will?"

He shook his head. "You'd better let them get settled first."

"Really?" Maude's face fell. One of the mares came over and nuzzled Becky's knee. She acted as if she wanted to make friends.

"Oh, yeah," Becky said to Will. "They look real upset to me." The horses walked around the paddock, curious about their new surroundings. They drank water from the trough and ignored the hay.

"They don't have a big butt like a quarter horse," J.J. pointed out. "How about that."

Will turned to him. "Are you going to ride one of them?"

"Beats looking at them," he said.

"The ladies are going to be so pleased," Maude declared.

"What ladies?"

"You met everyone, I think."

"From yesterday? What does that have to do with these Peruvian animals?"

She patted his arm. "We're going to ride them, dear. And now J.J. and Decker and the others will be able to ride more comfortably."

He shot a glance at Malone, who nodded. "We've heard it's just like sitting in a rocking chair," the old man said.

Great. He'd had three offers on the ranch already, and not one buyer had asked for fancy expensive horses to go with it. "What's wrong with sitting in an actual rocking chair, then?"

Everyone ignored him.

BECKY KNEW IT was coming, though she sure didn't look forward to it. But this was Will Cody's ranch now, and he could do as he pleased. Though why he would want to get involved was anybody's guess.

"I'd like to speak with you," the man had said. "In the office. Now."

"Sure," she'd said, trying to act as though she wasn't terrified of being fired. She'd hopped down from the fence and followed him into the west wing of the house. She checked her watch. It was time to check on the kids and relieve Decker of his little charges. She usually spent the afternoon in the house.

He lowered himself gingerly into his uncle's chair, then sighed as if every bone in his body hurt.

"How's your knee?" she asked, almost feeling sorry for him.

"I've had worse injuries," he said, picking up a sheaf of papers from the file marked *June*. "I haven't had a chance to look these over, but do you want to tell me how much my mother spent on those horses?"

Becky sat down in the chair on the other side of the desk. "Five thousand for the mares, six for the stallion."

"Apiece?"

"Yes."

He tossed the folder down, then took off his hat and tossed it on a nearby chair. "My mother has no business setting up a horse-breeding business."

"They're a good investment."

He ignored her words. "She shouldn't be riding at all. It's too dangerous."

"I think you'll have to take that up with her."

"I will."

"Is there anything else? I have work to do." She stood. "You'll find the books in order. Maude keeps track of the accounts."

"Where did thirty-one thousand dollars come from? I thought my uncle plowed every cent he had into buying property."

"You'll have to ask your mother about that."

"I intend to." He shook his head and muttered, "Thirty-one thousand dollars," then looked at Becky again. "Does the roof still leak?"

"Only when it rains," she quipped. He didn't smile.

"And the horse barn is still shored up on the northeast corner?"

She nodded. "And the pipes freeze in the bunkhouse and the plumbing here in the house is temperamental, the floors are cold, the heating system is ancient and the house needs rugs or carpet. Your mother's mattress is so old that it sags in three places and I keep throwing pans out because there are holes in the bottoms. The refrigerator is new, but the stove has been repaired twice, can't take much more, and—"

"Stop." He held up his hand as if to ward off her words. "In other words, thirty-one thousand dollars could have been spent differently."

"It's a business investment," Becky said. "You have to spend money to make money."

"And a fool and his money are soon parted."

Becky hesitated, but decided she'd better find out where she stood. "Are you staying here to run this place?"

"No."

"Do I have a job?"

"What makes you think you can run a ranch, Mrs. McGregor?"

"I've been doing it for the past six months," she replied. "Not that you would have noticed, you being on the road and all."

"That's how I make my living."

"And I make mine here," she reminded him. "Taking care of things for your mother."

"You still have a job. For now." He gave her a level look. "I'm putting the ranch up for sale."

She felt the blood drain from her face. "You can't do that."

"I think I can," he replied coolly.

"But it's been in your family for years."

The argument didn't seem to impress him. "You can stay until the place is sold. Maybe longer, if the new owner decides to keep you on."

"Does Maude know about this?"

"We haven't had a chance to talk."

"She might have something to say about your selling her home out from under her."

"This was my uncle's home. He never let either one of us forget it, either." Then, looking embarrassed that he had said too much, he returned his attention to the papers in front of him.

Becky turned and hurried from the office. She could have wished for a better answer, but she promised herself that no self-centered, irresponsible rodeo rider was going to take her dream away.

TOMMY SANG TO HIMSELF as he played with his bowl of orange gelatin. Becky had fed the boys and set out leftovers for the men in the bunkhouse kitchen. They liked to take the noon meal out there, but she made them come inside for supper. It was just too much work to cook two meals in two kitchens and besides, she and Maude liked the chance to talk over the day's work with the men while they ate.

Maude fixed herself another glass of iced tea and sat at the table reading the Sunday paper, since she hadn't gotten around to it yesterday. She folded it shut and turned to Becky. "That was a good party, wasn't it?"

"Definitely. I think everyone had a good time," Becky assured her.

"Will didn't come out for lunch."

"He's still in the office trying to figure out your bookkeeping system." He'd been in there for over an hour, which was keeping him out of her hair. Will's dog sat politely by Peter's chair and waited for scraps to drop on the floor. Peter pretended to drop them by accident. The animal eagerly gobbled them up.

"She likes potato chips," the boy said. "Weird, huh?"

"Don't give her too many. They might make her sick."

"Okay." He dropped a piece of beef from his sandwich. "Do dogs eat kittens? Do you think she'd hurt the kittens if she saw them?"

"I don't think so." She looked up from mixing meat loaf in a large pottery bowl. "That dog doesn't look mean, but the kittens' mother might have something to say about a dog looking at her babies."

Maude didn't look happy. "I really don't want Will going over the accounts."

Becky's eyebrows rose as she glanced toward her boss. "Why not?" She tried to tease her into a smile. "You haven't been stealing the profits, have you?"

But the woman didn't smile. In fact, she looked guilty. "Not exactly, but William's not going to like it."

"Do you want to tell me why not?" She dumped the meat loaf into two large loaf pans and patted it smooth, then washed her hands. Maude drank her iced tea and waited for her to sit down at the table before she spoke.

"He's been sending me money for years," Maude said, keeping her voice low.

"He has? Well, that's nice," Becky said, looking at the boys. She didn't know how much longer they'd be quiet. The baby concentrated on putting gelatin on his finger and sticking it in his mouth while Peter fed the dog his sandwich.

Maude nodded. "He's been very...generous. He's going to find out I didn't spend it and then he's going to find out that I did and then he's not going to be happy."

It took a moment to follow that one. "Did you spend it or not?"

"I spent it." Maude sighed. "But not on what he wanted me to spend it."

She couldn't imagine Maude gambling or drinking, though she liked to send in the contest entries she got in the mail. "What did you spend it on then?"

"Well, for one thing, the new horses."

"Thirty-one thousand dollars? That was the money your son sent?"

"Oh, there was lots more. He'd always send me money when he won. He kept trying to get me to move off the ranch and get a place in Billings, but I couldn't leave."

"Why not?" From everything she'd heard, Maude's brother had not been the nicest person in the world.

"My brother took me and Will in when we had nothing. I owed him for that. He gave us a home. I couldn't walk out and leave him alone when we both got old, could I? It wouldn't have been right. And what would I do in Billings?"

"Did your son understand that?"

"No."

"But J.W. left him the ranch."

"It was only fair, but Will's not going to understand any of this."

Becky patted her hand. "Sure he will. You're his mother. How can he be angry with you?"

"Well, even if he is, he'll have good reason. But he's like his father, who never had much of a temper either. Takes him a long time to get riled up, then watch out." The older woman finished her iced tea and stood up. "Guess I'd better take my nap. It doesn't look like Will's coming out of that office anytime soon, and if I'm sleeping I can put off talking to him."

"Not so fast, Mother," Will said, entering the kitchen. He had a sheaf of papers in his hand and he looked as if he could chew nails. Becky decided this would be a good time to take the boys upstairs and put Tommy Lee down for his nap, so she stood up and went to the sink. She kept a cloth there for cleaning the baby's face, so she dampened it with warm water and watched Maude sit back down in her chair.

"I really need my nap," the older woman said. "I'm seventy-four now."

"I know how old you are, Mother." He walked past the high chair without seeing the baby, but he nodded toward Peter. "Hey, kid. They give you any cake today?"

"It's for supper," the boy said.

"So this is where Lady went to. I wondered—"

"Daddy!"

Everyone looked at the baby. His eyes were round, his face covered with orange goo, and he was gazing rapturously at Will Cody.

"Who's that?" Will said, stopping to stare at the child.

"My brother."

"Tommy Lee," Becky said.

"Isn't he darling?" Maude asked.

"Daddy, daddy, daddy," the little boy chanted. He lifted his arms as if he expected Will to pick him up. Becky hurried over to him and started cleaning him up. She washed his face, then his pudgy hands. "I'm sorry," she said to Will, as she lifted her son into her arms. He was getting bigger every day, and she didn't know where he'd heard the word *daddy.* It wasn't like he'd ever had one. "He's never done this before. I don't—"

"Daddy," Tommy said, stretching toward the cowboy.

"I'm not your daddy," Will insisted, setting the papers on the table. He turned to Becky. "Tell him I'm not his daddy."

"That's not your daddy, honey. That's Mr. Cody, come to visit Miss Maude." But the child would not be denied. Almost knocking Becky off-balance, Tommy flung his arms out to the tall cowboy who had no choice but to open his arms and take the boy.

Tommy grinned and hugged him.

"I'm sorry," Becky said, trying to pry her son from Will with no success. "He's never done anything like this before."

Peter looked disgusted. "He's a baby."

Maude took the opportunity to quietly push back her chair and tiptoe from the room. Becky saw her go, but Will had his back to his mother as he bent over to set the little boy on the floor.

"No," Tommy said, hanging on. Will looked helplessly at Becky.

"What do I do now?"

"I'm sorry," she said again, reaching for her son. "I don't know what's gotten into him."

"Never mind," Will said, holding the child awkwardly. Tommy grinned and patted his face.

"He's tired," Becky said. "He's been playing all morning and . . ."

"Who takes care of the children while you're outside working?"

"Decker, J.J. and Oatey take turns."

"They don't mind?"

"No, I think they like it." She reached for Tommy, who suddenly decided that he would go into his mother's arms without a protest. He grinned at Will with a happy smile. "I'd better take him upstairs."

"My daddy died," Peter said, answering the unspoken question. "A long time ago, when I was two."

"I'm sorry." He looked at Becky with an oddly sympathetic look she didn't expect to see.

"Thanks."

Peter bent over and petted Lady's head. "I sure like your dog."

"She likes you, too."

"Think so?"

"Yeah." He looked past Becky to his mother's empty chair. "Where did she sneak off to?"

"To rest."

"Isn't she feeling well?"

"She's fine," Becky assured him, shifting Tommy on her hip. He was growing heavier every day. "She rests every afternoon. She says it gives her enough energy to stay up and see David Letterman after the news."

He sighed. "Go take care of your kids, Becky. I'll talk to my mother later."

"Okay." She hesitated before leaving the kitchen. "You know, she really is happy here."

"I find that hard to believe."

"Maybe you'd better look around. It might not be the same place that you left. And your mother might not be the same woman."

"Nothing's changed," he insisted, his mouth thinning into a straight line. He was still handsome, of course, even when he looked angry. "This place will never change, except to get older and shabbier."

There was no arguing with him. The old house wasn't in the greatest condition, but it had a certain personality. A few coats of paint and some insulated windows could do wonders. "Dinner's at six. If you need anything, talk to Decker or Cal. They're in charge in the afternoon."

He nodded. She left him pulling out a chair and sitting down at the table with the stack of papers he'd brought with him. If he wanted to sell the ranch, he could. The sad part about that was there wouldn't be anything she or Maude could do to stop him.

"I'M NOT LEAVING," Maude told her son. "If you've come to take me to Billings you can just forget that idea."

He looked up from his supper and stared at her. The ranch hands looked at each other and back down at their plates. Becky reached for the saltshaker.

"Maybe this isn't the time to talk about it," the young woman suggested. Will agreed. He didn't want an audience when he and his mother had this particular conversation.

"You can sell it out from under me, of course," Maude added.

"Let's not—"

"You can turn us all out into the street with nothing but our horses and our saddles and—"

"Mother," he tried again. He put down his fork. Everyone at the table looked at him like he was the devil himself. "I never—"

"That's what you came for," she said, a little sigh breaking her voice. "I heard in town today that you put the ranch up for sale and there was some interest in it from that big development east of Bozeman. And I'm not going. This is my home."

"It was my uncle's home."

"And mine." She lifted her chin defiantly, and Becky stood up and started to clear the table. The old cowboys looked as if they wanted to run out the door.

"Excuse me," the young woman said. "I'll put coffee on."

"Sit down, Becky," Maude continued. "I won't have all that dish clatter right now, if you don't mind." Becky sat. Maude looked at the ranch hands. "You'd better stay, too. This concerns our futures, all of us."

Peter turned to Will. "You in trouble?"

"I guess I am, but I sure can't figure out why," he said, looking down the length of the table to his mother. For some reason, he'd ended up with Peter on his left and the little one in the high chair on his right. Becky sat next to the baby and supervised his dinner. It was pretty much a disaster, but the dog would clean up the scraps from the floor. "I thought you wanted to move in with me when you didn't have to take care of J.W. anymore. We've talked about that off and on for years."

"*You*'ve talked about it," his mother said. "I've decided I don't like the idea."

"And why not?" He pushed his plate away. "What's wrong with the idea?"

"Well, for one thing, Billings is too big."

"You seem to enjoy it when you come to visit."

She looked at him as if he didn't know a steer from a bull. "It's different when you're on vacation, Willie. That doesn't mean I want to live there for the rest of my life."

"You can't stay here."

"Of course I can."

"You can't run a place this big."

"Why not?"

"It's too much work."

"Oh, pooh. I've been working all my life."

"And that's my point," he roared, losing his temper. "It's time for you to take it easy!"

"I don't want to." The look in those dark eyes dared him to argue with her.

Becky tried standing again. "I really think that this is a family discussion," she told Maude.

"I thought we should get it out in the open. We're all wondering what's going to happen, now that Will owns the ranch." She looked at her son. "If you've made any decisions, I hope you intend to reconsider." Her tone was formal, as if she was talking to a banker.

"I'd planned to sell."

There was silence as all eyes turned to him with expressions of surprise, resignation, disappointment and confusion.

"I'd planned to stay," his mother countered.

"You're trying to make me out to be some sort of monster. It won't work."

"Mon-ster!" Tommy called, and banged his fist on the tray of the high chair.

"Shh," Becky said. "Be good."

"You're seventy-four years old," Will continued. "Why would you want to spend the rest of your life on this godforsaken ranch?"

He was horrified when her eyes filled with tears. "It's my home," she said, her voice quavering. "I thought you'd come home, too."

"I can't," Will said, standing up and tossing his napkin on the table. He shot Becky an apologetic look. "I'll skip dessert," he said. "Thanks for supper."

He grabbed his hat on his way out the back door, and let the screen door bang shut behind him. Once outside, he took a deep breath and headed toward the corral. Lady fell into step beside him.

"Guess you're the only one talking to me, huh, girl?"

She wagged her tail and trotted alongside him as he crossed the wide dirt yard. Damn it, he hadn't come back to the Silver Valley to be yelled at.

4

"I'M TIRED OF BEING bossed around," Maude said, looking around the table. "Someone's been telling me what to do all my life." Becky put a plate of cookies on the table and handed Maude a mug of coffee. "Doesn't anyone understand that?"

"We understand," Becky told her, watching the cowboys look as if they wanted to be anywhere else on earth besides in the kitchen with an angry woman. "Anyone else for coffee?"

Decker stood first, and the other three followed. "Thanks for supper," Decker said, and there was a similar murmur from the others. "We'll just be on our way. Gotta check on the horses."

"Sure," Becky said, trying to keep a straight face as the men hurried out the door. They were tough men who could deal with just about anything on the ranch, but women confused them. "I'll be out later."

"Cowards," Maude muttered, after the screen door banged shut. "All of them, cowards. Except for the one I gave birth to. He turned out to be just plain crazy."

Becky turned to Peter. "You can go play on the porch, honey."

"Okay." He scooped a pile of action figures from the counter and headed for his favorite spot on the ranch. The wide porch that ran along the front of the house was safe from horses and cows. He'd learned the hard way that horses could step on toys and that would be the end of the toy.

"Me, too," Tommy demanded, holding his arms up.

"Pretty soon," his mother said. She started clearing the table. "After I finish here."

"I'll help," Maude said. "Just give me a minute to cool off."

"Well, you sent him running," Becky said. "He didn't look too pleased."

"Imagine, trying to get me to move away from here! Bossing me around. All my life men have told me what to do. Someone else has always known what's best for me." Becky stacked the empty plates into a pile. "And that doesn't mean they were right, either."

"It just means your son cares about you," Becky said. Despite everything, she had to give him credit for that. "Maybe we can't manage this place by ourselves, Maude. We've only been doing it for six months and you know we've been real busy. Some days it's hard to keep up. Some *weeks* it's hard to keep up."

"*You* think I should let him sell this place?"

"Of course not, Maude. I love it here, too, and I'm grateful to you for giving me the chance to work. But you can't blame your son for wanting you to take it easy, buy you a nice house, take care of you."

"Yes, I can."

"All right, have it your way." She set the stack of dishes in the sink and started loading the dishwasher. "I don't want him to sell either. What will we do with the horses?"

"We'll find ourselves another ranch," Maude said. "We'll take the men and the horses and we'll start over."

"We'd never be able to afford it," Becky argued. "We're not even making ends meet in this place, and that's without a mortgage to pay."

"We'll think of something. It's just that nothing's going to have the atmosphere that this place has."

"Maddie, Maddie," Tommy chanted. "I wanna get down!"

Maude moved over to a chair closer to the baby. "Here," she said, giving him a cookie. "Your mama will be all yours in just a minute." She turned to Becky. "I remember when Will was this size. Seems like a hundred years ago, though."

"What kind of baby was he?"

"Smart. Noisy." Maude shook her head. "He wasn't what you'd call a patient child."

And Becky didn't think he'd changed. He looked like a man who was used to getting his own way. No wonder he was a champion rodeo rider. The man was going to do what he wanted to do no matter what anyone or any animal had in mind otherwise. He'd met his match in Maude, though. Like mother, like son.

"He was like his father," Maude continued. "Handsome and stubborn and kind."

Kind? Becky put the dirty loaf pans in the sink and filled them with soapy water. She'd attack them later, after the sun went down. "How long were you married?"

Maude sipped at her coffee and made a face at Tommy, who giggled. "Eleven years. Will was nine when we moved here. We'd had a place east of here, but after Matthew died, well, I just couldn't hang on to it. The bank owned it all anyway, and they weren't about to let a woman have anymore money. So we moved in with my brother. And—" Maude sighed "—he wasn't the easiest person to live with. He did a lot of wrong things, made a lot of mistakes. But he managed to hang on to his ranch, and he took care of us, so I can't complain."

Becky dampened a washcloth and went to the high chair. Tommy protested the cleaning, but smiled when she was finished. "So handsome!" she told him, and he laughed.

"That's one good baby," the older woman affirmed.

"Yes, I've been lucky." Lucky she didn't miscarry after Jack died, lucky Maude had come to her rescue when she did.

"You do a good job with these children," Maude said. "It's not easy to raise a son alone. I should know."

"TROUBLES, SON?"

"What do you think?" Will sat in a rusted pickup truck parked behind the horse barn and looked at Decker. He motioned toward the passenger side, and the old cowboy accepted the silent invitation to sit inside. The passenger windows had been knocked out long ago, the tires were flat and the seat cracked and sagging, but Will didn't care. It was his truck and he'd sit in it any damn time he wanted.

"Your ma has strong opinions about staying here, I guess."

"Since when?" Will shook his head. "I've been talking about her moving in with me, and she's always said she couldn't leave J.W. Now that he's gone, I expected her to want to leave here as fast as she could."

"Women are strange creatures." He looked around the inside of the '62 Chevy. "They don't make 'em like they used to, do they?"

"You talking about trucks or women?" The men grinned at each other.

"Trucks, I guess," Decker drawled. "You used to come out here when you were a boy."

"This truck belonged to my father."

"Yeah."

"We used to do chores in it. He'd take me to town and I'd feel ten feet tall."

"You put up a fuss when J.W. wanted to sell it. He finally got disgusted and hauled it back here, where he couldn't see it unless he wanted to."

"He didn't have the right to sell it," Will said. "It was mine. Not his."

They sat in silence for a minute while Decker rolled himself a smoke, then patted his pocket for his matches.

"I guess that one hit close to home," Will said, while Decker lit his cigarette and rested his elbow on one bony knee.

"Yep. Guess a man don't have the right to sell what belongs to someone else."

"Trouble is, Deck, this place belongs to me now."

"Your ma doesn't think so."

"She's too old to run this ranch, Deck."

"Ain't we all, son," the old cowboy said, shaking his head. "Ain't we all."

"I couldn't stay past the summer," Will said.

"Wouldn't expect you to."

"And the ranch is still up for sale."

The old cowboy swallowed hard. "Guess nothing stays the same."

The two men sat in the abandoned truck for a while longer, as Decker finished his cigarette and Will tried to figure out just exactly what his mother was thinking. She'd always been tougher than she looked, he had to admit that. But, hell, he didn't want to stay here. The doctor had warned him to let the knee heal, or he'd be in serious trouble soon enough. It might be a good idea to stick around here and wait for Maude to change her mind, whether he wanted to or not.

"Why don't you stick around, son," Decker suggested, echoing his thoughts. "Jest for a while, of course. Till your ma comes to her senses. You should be a little nicer to the women, too. Otherwise you get beans for supper. And none of them chocolate chip cookies."

He grinned. "What kind of beans?"

"Maude'll get over being mad," the old cowboy promised. "She always does."

"I hope to hell you're right," Will said. "I feel like I'm eight years old and about to be paddled with one her wooden spoons."

"DON'T WORRY," Becky said, when Will approached her at the corral. She had Tommy by the hand, and the child immediately stretched toward Will. "Your mother will get over it."

"That's what Decker said, too," Will replied. He looked dejected, and she almost felt sorry for him.

"Then you'd better take our word for it." She really shouldn't feel sorry for him, she reminded herself. He'd brought it all on himself in the first place.

"Daddy," Tommy pleaded. "Pick me up."

Will frowned and looked at her. "Can you get him to stop calling me that?"

"Have you ever tried to reason with a toddler?" She looked down at the child and said, "This is not your daddy, honey."

Tommy Lee ignored her, and instead tugged at her hand and tried to go to the cowboy. "Pick me up *now*."

"Please," his mother added.

"Please," he said, breaking into a smile. Becky smiled, too. With his blond hair and blue eyes, he was a beautiful child. Peter was darker. His hair had turned slowly to chestnut, but Becky hoped Tommy would stay the way he was now. Will had no choice but to pick up the boy, and swung him easily onto his shoulders.

"Thanks," Becky said. He didn't look quite so intimidating with a child draped around his neck. The contrast was startling, with the man so dark, his face hardened into sharp planes and high cheekbones. Tommy was fair, with smooth pink skin and round cheeks. His chubby hands clutched the collar of Will Cody's denim shirt. "I'm afraid he likes to get his own way."

"Yeah. Well, you've got to give a man credit for trying."

Their eyes met. They both knew he wasn't talking about the child.

"You can't blame your mother for getting angry. Maybe you'd better stop giving orders," Becky suggested. "Otherwise no one on this ranch is going to be talking to you. Especially if the men keep missing out on dessert."

"What about you?"

She would have sworn he was trying to flirt with her. "What about me?"

"You're talking to me."

"Because I feel sorry for you. It must be hard to go through life making people angry."

"I think you have the wrong idea about me," he drawled. He almost looked as if he wanted to smile. "I'm not the jerk you think I am."

"Prove it."

His eyebrows rose. "How?"

"Stay here and help out. See what we're doing here before you decide to sell the ranch right out from under us. Your mother has big plans for the summer. Let her enjoy herself. She's having fun, for the first time in her life. Do you really want to put a stop to it?"

Will frowned. "I don't think you're in any position to give me advice. Not when it's your job at stake."

"I can get a job anywhere, Mr. Cody. I'm a first-rate cook and a first-rate foreman." She put her hands out and took her son down from Will's shoulders. "I happen to like your mother."

"And you don't like me."

She couldn't argue with the truth, so Becky didn't try. "I don't even know you. I *do* know that your mother is a real sweet woman. She's seventy-four years old and she wants to ride horses and go on pack trips and have fun with her friends. We're trying to figure out how to make this place pay for itself. Is that too much to ask of you to give us a chance?"

"I'll think it over," he said, but she had no idea if he really meant it.

"You do that." Becky swung Tommy into her arms and settled him against her hip. "We could sure use the help."

He didn't say anything, but simply looked at her with those dark eyes of his. Becky turned away and headed to the barn to see the new horses. According to Cal, they were settling in just fine. At least something around here was content.

BECKY CHECKED TO SEE how the horses were doing. They were mild-mannered animals, as tame and gentle as had been promised. There weren't many in Montana yet, but in time there could be. She was dying to ride one and see for herself how their gait differed from that of a quarter horse. Maude had gone to the horse show with a couple of her friends this spring, since Becky had been content to stay home with the children. She didn't mind having the men watch the children a few hours at a time, but leaving the kids for a night was too much to ask of the aging cowhands. Maude returned and announced she'd found a horse she could ride. And she'd liked them so much she'd bought six, enough to start a breeding business that was supposed to supplement the ranch income.

"Are these horses supposed to make money or eat it?" Will's voice drawled behind her. Becky kept looking at the mare as Will stepped next to her at the entrance to the stall.

"They're supposed to make money," she answered. "Maude calls it 'diversification.' She says all the ranches are developing other ways to make money besides selling beef cattle."

He nodded. "Sounds like a good idea, but why South American horses? What's wrong with raising quarter horses?"

"Don't knock it till you've tried it."

"Have you?"

He'd caught her on that one. "Not yet, but tomorrow I'm going to put them through their paces and see what all the fuss is about."

"All right," Will said. "That's what we'll do."

"We?"

He smiled at her, and her heart flipped in the most alarming way. Becky told herself it was just because she hadn't been around a man under the age of seventy for months. Except for the vet, who was a nice enough man but didn't have much to say except "Hold her steady now," she didn't often get a chance to talk to anyone her own age.

"I've decided to stick around for a while, at least until my leg heals and I can talk some sense into my mother."

"Good." She stifled an inward sigh of relief. "Maude will be pleased."

"I'm still selling the ranch," he said.

So much for relief. She turned to him, with Tommy's head nestled against her neck. He was tired now, relaxed in her arms. "I guess you'll do what you have to do," she said. "But I hope you'll keep an open mind."

"I'd like to see some of the ranch tomorrow. You want to go over what needs to be done tomorrow?"

"After I put Tommy to bed, sure."

"Good." His gaze flickered to the child. "He's half-asleep."

"He's a creature of habit." She moved toward the door of the barn. "Your mother's probably on the porch, just in case you're looking for her."

He smiled again. "Think she'll talk to me?"

"If you tell her you're staying."

Will followed her out of the barn. "Women are all alike," he drawled. "They're only happy if you tell them what they want to hear."

It was only a short reprieve, Becky reminded herself, ignoring his teasing. She walked beside the tall man down the road toward the house where Peter played with his action figures and Maude read the latest issue of *Country Woman* magazine and planned the next gathering of her friends. It would be the same as it was every evening, except for the man walking beside her. He wanted to change everything, and he had the power to do it. But maybe, just maybe, he'd change his mind.

"COME HERE," Maude said, waving Decker over to the window. "Look at that!" She pointed to Will and Becky walking together toward the house. The baby looked sweet, resting sleepily against the young woman's neck. "They're walking together."

"Who is?" Peter said, looking up from the floor.

"Nothing," Maude said. "Grown-up talk." Peter turned back to his toys. He was used to grown-up talk.

Decker joined her at the window. "Maybe he decided to listen to me."

"About what?"

"About stayin' on for a while."

"He doesn't listen to anyone," Maude said. "Never did."

"They're not talking," Decker pointed out.

"Haven't you ever heard of 'companionable silence'?" Maude studied their expressions. "At least they're not fighting."

"The boy is really trying hard not to limp. That leg must hurt."

"Maybe he's hurt too bad to rodeo."

"Could be. Or could be he'll be right as rain in a couple of weeks. He's made quite a name for himself, that boy has."

"Come away from the window," Maude said, backing up. "They'll see us."

"Yes, ma'am." The cowboy sighed. "Though I don't know what diff'rence that would make."

She sat down in her favorite overstuffed chair and picked up a magazine. "I don't want them to think that I'm—" She stopped. "Little pitchers have big ears."

"Yeah. I know what you're doing. I just think you're crazy, that's all." Decker took another cookie from the plate and sat down on the swing. He rocked himself while he ate. "Things just ain't that simple."

"We'll see," Maude said. "I have a few things up my sleeve, but everyone has to help. These children need a you-know-what and you-know-who needs a husband."

"You-know-who has her work cut out for her," Decker said.

"You're going to help me, aren't you?"

He reached for another cookie. "Yes, ma'am. Don't I always?"

Maude knew he only pretended to protest. None of them wanted to leave the ranch and try to find a new place somewhere else. She didn't intend to be shut up in some little house all by herself, while her son was on the road trying to break his neck. She didn't want to leave her new friends or her new horses or her home. And it was her home, no matter what Will thought. The boy didn't understand, and it was about time he settled down and took over what was rightfully his.

"Where is everyone?" Will hollered.

"Out here." She heard him clomp through the house, but when he stepped out onto the porch he was alone.

"Where's Becky?"

She pretended she was still mad at him. Which she was, sort of. "Putting the baby to bed, I guess. That girl works too hard."

"Good cook, too," Decker said. "You want a cookie?"

Peter looked up. "I do."

"Well, come over here and grab one before they're all gone." Peter took a cookie and, ignoring the adults, went back to the corner to play.

"I wondered where my dog went," Will said, sitting down next to Decker in the swing. He stretched out his legs and winced. "Now I know."

Lady looked up from her position next to Peter, then put her head back down and closed her eyes.

"She's found herself a boy," Decker said.

Will whistled for the dog, who didn't respond. It was as if Lady had suddenly gone deaf.

"She's sleeping," Peter told him. "You shouldn't wake her up."

Now he was being told what to do by a four-year-old. Hell, he should have stayed in Denver and taken his chances with the bulls. He turned to his mother and waited for her to say something. Anything. "I checked on the new horses," he tried. "They look like they're settling in."

She looked at him. "And what about you? Are you settling in?"

"No." Staying for the summer didn't mean settling down.

Maude sniffed. "The horses are smarter than you are."

"I didn't want to inherit this ranch," Will stated. "What ever happened to that cousin over in Great Falls?"

"J.W. fought with him, too. Said he wasn't worth the powder to blow him away."

"No wonder we didn't have any family around."

"I didn't have you until I was forty-one. My folks were gone, and your father's mother lived back East in a nursing home. There was no one left but me and J.W. He'd been living here alone for years, hiring a woman in the summer to cook for the crew." She flipped the page of her magazine and studied the pictures. "I don't want to discuss it anymore, William."

Becky stuck her head in the doorway. "Anyone want anything? I'm fixing myself a drink."

Will nodded. Maybe he could get used to being waited on. "I'll have a beer, if you've got one."

"Sure. What about you, Maude? The usual?"

"Not tonight, thank you. I guess I'm still worn-out from yesterday." She put her magazine on the floor and stood up. "I'll take Peter up with me."

"Thanks. Decker?"

"Uh, no, thanks, Reb." The old man stood up and moved toward the screen door. "The sun's gone down. Guess it's time to get to bed."

"Okay." She disappeared and Will turned to Decker. "Where is everyone?"

"Cal, Oatey and Malone were finishing up a while ago. I guess they're bedding down, too."

Maude went over to the little boy. "Come on, Peter. We'll say good-night to your mama and head up to bed."

The child looked as if he wanted to protest, but thought better of it. Lady started to get up, too, with the boy, but Will told her to stay.

"'Night," Peter told the men. "See ya tomorrow."

"Good night," Will said, and Decker waved goodbye as he went out the door and down the steps. Maude bent down and kissed Will on the cheek before she ushered the boy into the living room, so Will figured she couldn't still be upset with him. She wasn't the kind of person to hold a grudge. "I was hoping we could go over some ranch business," he said.

"Not tonight. Besides—" she yawned "—Becky will be able to tell you anything you need to know."

He should have expected that. It was too much to expect that there would be something that the pretty blonde wouldn't know anything about. The sky had grown darker outside, so he switched on a lamp, then went to the office to retrieve the pad of notes he'd made earlier. He might as well start acting like he owned the place. He would have to get the account ledgers in shape, make sure the breeding records were complete and the cattle inventoried. He went back to the porch and sat down, rocking slightly on the wood swing.

Becky returned, handed him a beer and sat down in Maude's chair. They both watched the dog walk past them out of the room.

"Thanks," he said, remembering his manners. "I guess I don't have to ask where she's going," Will said, turning to the woman across from him. She'd set her drink on the wide arm of the chair and crossed her legs. She was slim, he guessed, despite the jeans that looked too large. The belt that held them up was cinched as far as it could go. Her shirt was a faded blue check, the sleeves rolled up to reveal tanned arms. The long yellow braid of hair lay over her shoulder, touching the top of her left breast. She looked every inch the cowgirl, complete with freckles and a sunburned nose. She was pretty, in that outdoorsy way of Western women. He tried to imagine her wearing lipstick and a short dress and couldn't. It was hard to believe that she was old enough to have two kids.

"Petey likes animals and they tend to like him."

"Yeah, I can see that." He turned to watch his dog slink through the living room toward the main staircase. "I guess he's got himself a dog."

"Sorry."

Will shrugged. "Doesn't matter. She's getting too old to trail after me all the time."

Becky took a sip of her drink and nodded at the notepad. "I see you're not wasting any time."

"I have to know what's here."

"Two hundred twenty-seven cows, one hundred ninety-one calves, fifty heifers, twelve Hereford bulls and nineteen horses, counting the ones that arrived today. We didn't breed the yearling heifers this month."

"Why not? That's a big loss in calf production."

"Yes, but it's labor-intensive. We all just about killed ourselves this spring trying to deal with the problems yearlings have giving birth. I just don't have the manpower for it."

"That's risky," was his only comment.

"Maude and I decided that this way we could handle what we have."

"Have you made any other changes that I should know about? Besides starting a fancy South American horse-breeding business and cutting down on calves?"

She took another sip of her drink. "No. I've just been trying to keep up with what J.W. had set up, though he'd let things slide over the years."

"What about artificial insemination? I don't see any records."

Becky shook her head. "Your uncle believed in breeding the old-fashioned way, but that's something you might want to investigate for next year, if you're here. The heifers are separate, in the north section."

"I'd like to see them."

"We can ride out tomorrow. Anything else?"

"Not right now."

"Okay." She leaned her head back against the chair cushion and closed her eyes. He couldn't help looking at her. She looked very young and very tired. A widow, they'd told him. She couldn't have been married very long.

"Do you mind my asking how old you are?"

She answered without opening her eyes. "Twenty-eight going on fifty."

"This is a hard life for a woman," he muttered. "Why don't you want to live in town?"

"I like it here." She didn't look at him. Instead she finished her drink and stood up. "If you'll excuse me, I'm going to bed. Five-thirty comes early."

"Sure. See you in the morning."

"Good night."

She left Will alone on the porch. It hadn't changed much. There was still a stack of magazines in between the chairs and the inexpensive Charles Russell prints on the wall. There were a few tears in the screen, and the wood floor needed a fresh coat of khaki paint, but it was pretty much just like he remembered. His uncle had added it to the front of the house when Will was thirteen. Unlike Peter, he hadn't had time to sit down and play in the corner, that's for sure. He'd been treated like one of the hands from the time he could swing his leg over a horse. He'd been expected to do the work of a man, and he'd done it without complaining.

Until that one night when all hell broke loose. Will drained his beer and put it out of his mind. He had to think of the future now, had to decide what was best for everyone. He'd stay for as long as he had to and no longer.

His knee started to ache, but Will decided against taking any painkillers. He'd stick with the beer and a good night's sleep. Lord, it was quiet out here. The porch swing squeaked a little, but that was the only sound. He was used to crowds and excitement. He was used to competition and honky-tonk bars and eating dirt when a bronc pitched him off its back. He was up for Rodeo Rider of the Year for the second time, and if his knee hadn't wrenched apart, he'd have been sure to win it. He couldn't turn his back on all that and become a man who went to bed at nine and got up at five and worried about rain.

The problem was, he just couldn't imagine living on the Silver V and not going stark raving mad. He'd been forced to live here when he was a skinny nine-year-old kid, but he was almost thirty-four, and no one could make him stay one day longer than he had to.

5

BECKY LOVED her bedroom, with its simple painted iron bed and old yellow starburst quilt. The dresser was oak, the bathroom right across the hall. The upstairs held faded green rugs: its walls were painted ivory. Maude had been right to keep the ranch house simple and uncluttered. Downstairs, in the living room and kitchen, there was enough junk for five families. She missed having a home of her own, but she also knew how lucky she was to have had someplace to live and work, with the children with her.

She loved the nights, loved the few minutes alone at the end of each day when her children were sleeping and the house was quiet. She could soak her tired body in the deep tub and pretend that she could sleep late in the morning. That would be a luxury indeed. When she was done with her bath, she'd put on a light cotton nightgown, check the boys one last time and then patter back to her own room and climb into bed. The alarm would be set for five o'clock; morning always seemed to come too soon. But tonight there was a dog at the foot of Peter's bed and there was a man downstairs; she could hear his footsteps as he walked around the kitchen. He had come to change everything, to sell the ranch and take Maude away. He hadn't thought of what would happen to the men. Didn't anyone wonder what happened to old cowboys who couldn't work anymore? She would have to show him that the ranch was running well, that they could take care of it, that it wasn't too much work for Maude. He could go back to his rodeo life and whatever else he did.

It would be better if he stayed, of course. It would be better to have a strong young man giving orders and making decisions and doing the work that required muscles. She could go back to cooking and playing with her kids and doing what she was hired to do. Will could make the decisions and Maude could have her horses and her friends, with no worry about the day-to-day problems of the cattle business.

Will Cody was nice when he wanted to be. He'd been nice enough to hold Tommy and talk to Peter. He hadn't even seemed to mind too much when his dog abandoned him. He was probably a nice man, Becky decided, snuggling into her pillow. His problem was that he wasn't smart enough to know where he belonged.

THE KITCHEN SECTION of the bunkhouse was the only area Becky ever entered. The bunkhouse itself was old, a leftover from the early 1900s. It was a long narrow building, similar to a motel. Every room had its own front door, and there was a communal bathroom at the back. The kitchen was sparse, but held a large square table, eight scarred wooden chairs, and the usual kitchen equipment lined one wall. The men made their own breakfast and lunch, with Becky seeing that they had enough food on hand. She met the men there most mornings and went over the plans for the day.

"Good morning."

Becky turned around from her conversation with J.J. and Cal and glanced over at Will. "Good morning."

"Are we riding or driving?" Will nodded first to her, then to the two men. "Looks like it's going to be a good day."

"Either way," she said. "It doesn't make any difference to me."

"We'd better take a truck," he declared. "I don't think I can sit a horse yet."

"Okay." Better, in fact. That way she'd get back to eat lunch with the kids. Maude was watching them this morning, and she and Becky planned to ride the Peruvians this afternoon and see what they could do. Becky had gotten up early, done her chores in the horse barn and grabbed a peanut butter sandwich for breakfast. Maude, nearly bursting with excitement, had decided to work in her garden. Tommy liked to make mud pies and Peter liked to water the plants, so it would work out for all three of them. She'd asked Maude if she wanted to go with her son instead, but the woman had looked at her as if she'd lost her mind.

Now she turned back to the men, whose work for the day would include working with the new horses and making sure the machinery was ready for haying season. Somebody was always driving to town for parts these days. Will stood beside her and acted as though he was listening, then they walked past the sheds and corrals to where an assortment of vehicles was parked.

"Where are we going?"

"We can start over at the Second Meadow and check the cows there. Cal said there're a few he's keeping an eye on, and I want to make sure the calves are okay."

"Do you want to drive?" he asked her, hesitating before opening the driver's door.

"Go ahead," she said. "The key's inside."

"That hasn't changed," he said, getting in the truck. "But not much has."

"Your uncle wasn't much for change," Becky said. "He wouldn't even let me experiment with supper. He wanted the same foods, and he wanted them the way he'd always had them."

"Yeah," Will said, bitterness in the word. "I know. He was one hell of a pain in the ass."

"Well," Becky conceded, trying to be tactful. "He wasn't the easiest man in the world to get along with. I don't think he had any friends."

"No," Will said, guiding the truck across the field toward the fence. "I imagine that by the time he died he didn't have a friend left to mourn him."

"Quite a few came to the funeral, actually. Out of respect for Maude, I suppose," Becky said, remembering that cold October day. It had been impossible to stay out of the wind, and back at the house she'd prepared gallons of coffee for the frozen guests. "You were in Europe then, weren't you?"

"Yeah. Germany's crazy about rodeos. I did a couple of exhibitions and some judging. Maude told me not to bother coming back to pay my respects." He glanced over at her. "You probably think I was wrong to listen to her."

"I mind my own business." Becky hopped out when they reached the gate and swung it open. That was one disadvantage to being the passenger. There were always gates to open and close anywhere you went. When she got back in the truck after closing the gate behind them, she was surprised that Will continued the conversation. She'd expected him to be quiet. She hadn't expected him to act like she knew what she was doing.

"I would have been a hypocrite to go to that funeral and mourn that man."

She braced her hand on the dashboard as they went over a rough spot and turned to look at him. "It was that bad?"

"Yeah."

"But he left you the ranch. That must count for something."

"That's the part I can't figure out," the man said slowly. "That's what makes no sense, no matter how much I try to figure it. He should have left it to Maude, but I guess he figured she couldn't run it."

"And you could."

He laughed, but there was no humor in the sound. "I could run it, all right, but I'd just as soon rope an elephant."

"I don't get it," Becky said. "Most people would be turning cartwheels if they ended up owning a ranch this size."

"And up to their ears in debt and hard work," he added.

"I don't—"

"That's a pretty big price tag," Will muttered.

She'd been about to say that she didn't think the ranch was in debt like most operations. It didn't make much money after expenses, of course. And some months were worse than others. She and Maude had spent a long winter trying to figure out how they could get a little extra income.

They traveled north, past groups of Hereford cows and calves. They were pretty cattle, various shades of brown with white markings. The animals looked up from their grazing for a second, but then returned to what they were doing.

"Good-looking animals," Will said.

"You sound surprised."

"I didn't know what to expect," he admitted. "I don't know how you've done this all by yourself for the past six months, that's all."

"We all work hard."

"Did you have much trouble with the calving?"

"Some." It had actually been six weeks of almost non-stop work. Keeping track of more than two hundred mothers and babies had at times seemed close to impossible. "We lost one calf to cold, two more drowned in the creek before we found them. The usual. We had about ten calves in the sheds at any one time. They took a lot of nursing."

"And you wonder why I want to sell out," he murmured. "This is a hard life, all right."

"It's my job," Becky said, wondering if she could make him understand. "I started out cooking and cleaning for your mother. I sure didn't intend to be managing this operation. I don't know what I would have done without the men. Decker can tell if a cow is going to calf by the look in her eye and J.J. knows everything there is to know about horses. Cal likes tinkering with machinery, and Oatey is good with kids and calves."

"And the summer camp?"

"No one's run cattle up there for years."

He frowned. "Why not? That was good grassland."

She shrugged. "Not enough help, I guess. And we're not running enough stock either."

"I take it my mother hired back the men J.W. fired over the years."

"Yes."

He stopped the truck and turned to her. "Why?"

"She says she's making amends for all the wrong that's been done." She wished Will Cody wasn't quite so handsome, or so close to her. It was unnerving sitting beside him, and she wasn't sure why. She worked with men all day long, and yet she never experienced this self-conscious, run-like-hell feeling that made her want to leap out of the truck and disappear behind the next rise.

He shook his head and smiled to himself. "I should have known she'd do something like that."

"Yes. She's a very loyal person." She needed to get out more. She needed to go to town and be around people, not cattle and kids and old men. The next time the veterinarian was out at the ranch, she'd say yes if he asked her out. He'd done that awhile back, when she was covered with manure and mud, but she'd thought he was kidding. Until he'd asked her again, a few weeks later, and she'd said no because Tommy was sick and she didn't want to leave him.

Will put the truck in gear and continued and the conversation stopped. They found the cow Decker had warned her about and inspected her. She and her calf seemed fine, so Deck would be relieved. To Becky's surprise, Will knew a lot about cows and seemed at ease out in the pasture. They drove for hours, checking fence and looking for trouble, until the sun was high overhead.

"Must be around noon," Will said.

Becky looked at her watch. "Yep. I have to get back to the kids, and I wanted to be around when Maude rode one of the new horses this afternoon."

"Can we keep going and end up at the house?"

"No. I guess there used to be a road, but it washed out years ago. You'll have to go back the way we came." He turned the truck around, and Becky hopped in and out to open and close the gates. "We should have brought

Pete with us," she said. "He's just about tall enough to do this job."

"He doesn't need to be out here," Will said. "He's too young to be working."

Becky turned to him in surprise. "I didn't say he was working. He just likes to ride with me and open gates."

"Leave him at home from now on." He shot a glance in her direction. "From the moment I set foot on this place, my uncle had me working. Seven days a week, before school and after school. All I'm saying is, let Peter be a kid for as long as he can. Growing up on a ranch is hard work."

"This is a good place to raise children."

He shrugged. "I guess that depends on who's doing the raising."

They rode back to the house in silence.

IT WAS WONDERFUL to see them together. Maude watched as the truck bounced across the field and parked by the garage. The young people had spent all morning together. She hoped they hadn't fought. She hoped they'd talked. Or kissed. But that was too much to ask. She reined in her horse and figured she'd settle for knowing they'd been in the same place all morning.

She nudged the mare and trotted toward them. It was like riding a couch cushion. None of her bones jarred or ached, nothing hurt. She felt as if she could ride for miles. She felt as if she were twenty again. Well, forty anyway.

"What the hell are you doing?" Will turned off the ignition and got out of the truck as his mother trotted over toward them.

"I think you can figure it out," Maude said. She tucked a strand of silver hair under her hat and smiled at her handsome son. She reached over and patted the mare's neck. "Isn't she a beauty?"

"You shouldn't be riding. Not with your arthritis." He walked over and greeted the horse, then took it by its bridle. Becky walked over and rubbed the horse's nose.

"Don't knock it till you've tried it," his mother chided.

"What's this one's name?" her future daughter-in-law asked.

"Duchess of York."

Will looked up. "What?"

Maude chuckled. "The mares are all named after royalty. Seems their sire is King Henry and the dam is Lady Catherine."

Becky chuckled. "Did you know that when you bought them?"

"Yes. We also have Princess Elizabeth, Lady Caroline, Countess Levien and Lady Jane."

Will looked at her as if she was losing her mind, but Maude decided to forgive him. "Let me guess," he drawled. "The stallion you bought is Prince Charles?"

"No. His name is Doug. He's from a different breeder."

"I can't wait to meet him," Will said, walking around the mare. She stood patiently as Will looked her over.

"Let's go then," Maude said. "I couldn't wait for you any longer."

Becky smiled. "I should have known. Where are the boys?"

"I gave them lunch. Oatey is with Tommy. I think they're both having a nap. And Peter's with Malone in the barn. They're saddling up the others."

"Is everything all right?"

Silly question, Rebecca. Everything was fine. Her son was home, her riding plans were going to work out, and she was going to have at least two beautiful grandchildren. "Oh, they were as good as gold. As always."

Her son gave her a questioning look. "What are you up to, Mother?"

"Can't a woman smile without someone thinking she's up to something?"

"No," he replied flatly. He turned to Becky. "Are we going to ride these royal nags or are we going to stand here?"

"We're going to ride, my lord," she quipped, looking especially pretty.

Ah, thought Maude, stifling a satisfied sigh. This was all going to work out after all.

DOUG TURNED OUT to be one hell of a horse. Will didn't think his knee or his back would be able to take more than thirty minutes on a horse, but the Peruvian stallion surprised him. No two hooves landed on the ground at the same time, a motion that gave a smooth ride without bouncing or jarring. Decker, Malone and Becky were on the other mares, who were all as well trained and obedient as the Duchess Something his mother was trotting around.

It was a world away from the rodeo.

"Do you think they've ever seen cows before?" he asked, reining in next to Becky. She was a good rider, with a balanced seat and light hands. She was on the smallest mare, though all the horses were a good size.

Becky motioned for Malone to open the gate. "I guess there's only one way to find out." His mother hadn't stopped smiling, Will noticed, which might mean that she was speaking to him again. The other men wore similar expressions, as though they couldn't believe what they were doing.

"I'll be switched," Decker said, nudging the mare through the gate. "If I didn't know I was on a horse I wouldn't know I was on a horse!"

"Are there any more of these in Montana?" Malone called to Maude.

"Only about sixty," she said, following Decker from the corral and toward the wide grasslands to the east. "But next year there'll be a few more."

"Meaning you still intend to breed them." He wondered if his mother lay awake nights trying to think up foolish things to do.

"Meaning my new business will be a success." She gave her horse a slight kick and trotted off to keep up with Decker, who was clearly enthusiastic.

Becky trotted up beside him. "You don't know when to quit, do you?"

"She has to be made to see reason."

"She's having fun."

"Ranches aren't for fun."

Her eyebrows rose. "Really. You look like you're having a pretty good time. And I don't see you doing any work around here. Why would you have anything to complain about?"

She was right, which ticked him off. There would always be plenty of work. A man could ride in any direction and there would be something to fix or something to feed. There would be a warm wind and the smell of hay and a hot yellow sun hanging in a big blue sky. There would never be enough hours in the day to do everything there was to be done. There would never be enough money or enough time or enough patience to wait until there was a profit at the end of the year.

"What do you do during the off-season of the rodeo?" Becky asked. "There is an off-season, isn't there?"

"Spring and fall."

"Well, where do rodeo riders go?"

"I have a place."

"A condo, ranch, house, trailer, what?"

He didn't know why she was so interested. "Twenty acres, enough to keep a few horses."

Her expression showed that she didn't think that twenty acres could compare to thirty thousand. They passed another broken section of fence. Will sighed. It would take ten men all summer to fix the fences.

"We need help with the haying," Becky said. "I know your knee is bad, but do you know anything about it?"

"Yeah," he said. He'd spent every summer as an unpaid member of the hay crew. He was sure J.W. regretted his sister not having more sons before her husband was killed. "I'll talk to Decker and see what needs to be done."

"Great. That's a load off my mind."

They rode in silence for a few more minutes, through a large meadow and a section of the ranch they hadn't covered this morning. Will looked around, surprised at the sparse number of cows and calves he saw grazing. "You said you're not using the summer pasture?"

"No."

"But you're not running as many cows as you could be. That's one of the reasons you're not making enough money."

"I don't have enough *anything*," she told him. "That's the problem. If you think you can handle things better, you're welcome to try." With that, she urged her horse ahead and trotted up to join the others who by now were far ahead of them. Well, he should have kept his mouth shut, but he couldn't figure out why there wasn't more stock. Had J.W. lost interest in ranching somewhere along the line? The place should have at least managed to break even, but the accounts he'd seen showed that it wasn't even doing that. But that was ranch life for you, Will mused. You could break your back all year and still have nothing to show for it. Unless you loved the life, which he didn't.

Still, it was good to be on a horse, even though his back was starting to ache. And it was good to be out under the vast blue sky and feel like his life was his own.

And there were some advantages, like watching Becky's shapely rear in the saddle. She had a fine figure, but Will wasn't getting anywhere near her. She was a woman with children, a woman who would want commitment and devotion. He hadn't been with a woman in six months, but he wasn't going to mess with Becky.

SHE SHOULDN'T HAVE lost her temper again, Becky fumed, taking the saddle from the chestnut mare. She should smile and be polite and agreeable. When on earth was she ever going to learn to keep her mouth shut? As soon as she finished rubbing down Lady Jane, Becky told herself that she was going to become a model of tact and diplomacy.

It wasn't going to be easy. She looked at her watch. After four already, and the boys would be wondering where she was. There was supper to fix, too. She'd have to use a couple of casseroles she'd put aside for the hay crew. At least she didn't have to clean. Luckily the house still looked good from the cleaning she and Maude had given it Sunday morning, for the party.

She stood apart from the others. Will, his limp more accented than this morning, took care of the Pasos stallion with grim determination written all over his face. He should be off that leg, but he wasn't going to admit it.

"You miss rodeoin'?" Malone asked him.

"Yeah."

Well, that was informative, Becky thought, shamelessly eavesdropping on the conversation a few yards away.

"I did a stint as a clown once," the older cowboy said.

"Yeah? When?"

"Years back. I wasn't any good at it," the old man drawled. "Besides, I didn't think that was a real smart way to make a livin'."

"It's all hard work," the younger man said, "whatever you do."

Malone's reply was muffled, but it sounded agreeable. Then, "This here's the perfect situation," he told Will. "A good-size spread, not too big and not too small. Enough water and enough flatland and plenty of rangeland. A man could settle down and make a fine life for himself and his sons here."

Becky hid her smile behind the horse. In his own way, the old cowboy was doing his part. But talking to Will Cody was like talking to the wind. You could say all you wanted and your words made no difference.

"WHO'S OSCAR REDDING?"

Maude looked up from her perusal of *Ranch Living* magazine. "Your uncle's lawyer. Why?"

"He called and left a message on the answering machine. Says he wants me to call and arrange an appointment."

"Must be something about the estate," Maude said.

Will shrugged. "I'll call him tomorrow. You and I should go over the records of the business. There are a number of things I don't understand."

Maude tossed her magazine on the sofa cushion beside her and stood up. "I suppose, but I don't know how much good I'll be to you. I'd better get Becky."

"No!" Maude gave him a questioning look, and Will added, "I think she's busy with the kids right now." He didn't want those big blue eyes looking at him and messing up his concentration. That's what happened last time and he'd ended up arguing with her instead of kissing her. He sure as hell wasn't about to do either one.

"Well," Maude sounded reluctant. "I guess."

He let her lead the way to the office, but Peter and Lady intercepted them in the hallway. The dog stayed close to the boy as if she thought Will was going to take her away. "You want to play checkers?"

"Me?"

The boy nodded. "Miss Maude taught me."

Will shook his head. "I don't think—"

"Sure you can," Maude said, pushing him forward. "We can have our meeting anytime. Petey here needs someone to play with and I'll go see if Becky needs help in the kitchen."

"She's cooking," the child said. "We're having something with cheese on top." He turned to Will. "Are you gonna play?"

Will was stuck. "Aren't you a little young for checkers?"

The boy looked surprised. "I don't think so."

"Play with him, Will," Maude said. "Remember how I used to beat you?"

"Don't believe her," he told the boy. "She always lost." Peter grinned and put his hand into Will's.

"Come on," the boy said. "The box is on the porch."

Will had no choice but to follow him. He remembered being small, vaguely remembered a tall dark-haired man with a quiet voice who had patiently played games. He wondered what his life would have been like if his father hadn't been killed. He wondered if Peter would think about that someday. No doubt he would and a small corner of his heart would be sad for what he never had. "All right," he told the boy. "Who gets to be red?"

WILL TRIED TO talk to Maude again after dinner, but the ranch hands needed help with the bunkhouse bathroom. It took most of the evening to fix the plumbing, and someone would have to go for parts in the morning so the shower would work. From the bunkhouse kitchen window he caught glimpses of Becky and the children walking around. She put them in the old station wagon and left. She probably went to town, maybe visited a friend.

"Does Becky have a man?" He turned away from the window and sat down at the battered table with the cowboys.

The four men stared at him. Decker grinned. "Now why would that be any of your business? You interested?"

He was sorry he'd spoken. He should have known better. Cowboys were terrible gossips and loved a good joke. They would tease him to death from now on, given half a chance. "No, of course not. I just wondered."

"Pretty woman," Malone offered, shuffling a deck of cards. "Too bad she doesn't have a husband."

"Why is that?" Will asked, figuring it was too late to stop the conversation anyway, so he might as well find out what the boys knew.

"Mebbee she's picky," Oatey offered.

Decker shrugged. "How's she going to meet anyone around here? She goes to town sometimes, to pick up what we need or get supplies, but it's not like she gets to meet anyone. Except Doc Thomas." He turned to Cal. "Did he ask her out?"

"Yeah. But she turned him down the first time. The second time, too, 'cuz the little one had the scours."

"Who's Thomas?"

"Doc Thomas, the vet. Nice fella," Decker said, looking at Malone. "Are we playing cards or are you just gonna sit there and shuffle 'em all night?"

"I'm talking," he said, slapping the deck on the table. "Will here wants to know about Miss Becky. 'Course it's about time he got his head out of his butt and saw what was right in front of him." He grinned at Will. "No offense, boss."

Will leaned back in his chair. "She's not my type," he declared, making the men howl with laughter. "What's so funny?"

"You are, son," Decker managed to say. "You've been giving her moony looks whenever you think no one's watching. And you frown at her all the time like she's driving you crazy." He chuckled. "I wouldn't know anything about your 'type,' but hell, son, she's a woman and you're a man."

"I figured that part out already." He smiled to show he took the teasing.

"Now, that's a good start," Malone drawled. "I heard figuring it out is the most important part." The men roared with laughter once again, and Will reached over and cut the cards.

"Are you going to play?" he asked. "Or are you just gonna sit here like a bunch of hyenas?"

"Five card stud," Oatey declared, setting a box of matchsticks on the table. "Count 'em out."

Malone began to deal. "Read 'em and weep."

Will picked up his cards as they were dealt. He was glad that the men were occupied with something else besides giving him advice about women. He didn't need to know anything more about women than that women and rodeo didn't mix.

6

"WE'VE GOT TO GET some of the stock up to the summer pasture," Will announced at breakfast. "I drove up there the other day and you're just letting good grass go to waste."

Becky set a platter of fried eggs next to the plate of bacon on the table. "You think it's worth the trouble?"

"Yeah." He helped himself to eggs and bacon, then sprinkled them liberally with salt and pepper. "I do. There are enough of us to do the job, I think, though it might take awhile."

Maude nodded. "I think that's a lovely idea. The ladies are coming out here this morning to see the new horses and take turns riding them."

"Not today," Will said. "I can't baby-sit your club and get any work done."

"You don't have to 'baby-sit' anyone," she said, helping herself to another piece of toast. She spread homemade apple butter on it and took a bite. "We're quite capable of taking care of ourselves, thank you."

Becky sat down with a mug of coffee. "The move to the summer pasture can certainly wait another day."

Will shook his head. "The weather is supposed to be good today, and then we'll have to get busy with the haying. You're not taking advantage of all the grazing land. That's probably one of the reasons why this place isn't making any money." Of course, employing four old men and an inexperienced foreman didn't help either, but he sure wasn't going to voice that opinion. The men worked as hard as they could and Becky did the work of three women, from what he could see.

Becky smiled at him, an unusual occurrence, he realized. "Then we can go to one of the auctions and pick up some more stock," she said.

"Why would *we* want more stock?"

"You just said yourself that we're not taking advantage of the grazing land that we have."

"That didn't mean I wanted to do anything about it. All I'm saying is that there's range that isn't being used."

"Aside from that," Maude interjected, "I think herding cows would be a wonderful thing for the Not Dead Yet Club to do today. I'm sure the ladies will be thrilled to get the chance to be helpful."

"The ladies?" Will said, turning away from the disconcerting blue eyes of Becky McGregor to stare at his mother. "Herding cows? No way."

"Why not?"

"Someone will get hurt."

"We'll all be careful," Maude insisted, turning to Becky for support. "You can drive the truck the back way and meet us there, with the children, for lunch."

"A picnic?" Becky offered. "What a great idea! You'll have to draw me a map. I'm not familiar with a lot of those roads."

The women turned to Will. "What time should we be ready?" Maude asked.

"Never," he muttered.

"They're coming at nine." She stood up and picked up her dirty dishes. "I'd better get my work clothes on." With that she left the table, putting her dishes in the dishwasher before leaving the room. Becky and Will sat in silence at the table for a few minutes longer.

"This won't work," he said finally.

She smiled again. "It *is* a little bizarre. But maybe it's actually a good idea. You need all the hands you can get. You can't deny that."

"But I'd like to." He couldn't resist smiling back at her. For days he'd tried to stay out of her way, which hadn't been easy since they ate two meals a day together.

"It will be fine. Just try to have a little patience."

"Patience?" That got to him. He'd played close to a hundred games of checkers in the past four days alone. The four-year-old kid was starting to beat him once in a while. "I'm the most patient man in Montana. What's so damned funny?"

"You are," she replied, standing up. "I have to go see if the kids are awake yet. It's going to be a busy morning."

"At least you get to stay here," he muttered.

"And you get to ride north with a dozen women."

"We don't have enough horses."

"Sure we do. Cal will stay here and work on the mower. I won't be riding. That leaves more than enough."

"If you say so."

She patted him on the shoulder. It was brief, but he found the touch of her hand disturbing. "You'll survive. And the cows will, too."

"How can you be so sure about that?"

Becky ignored him and disappeared up the back staircase, leaving him alone in the kitchen to brood about the day. What he'd planned as a necessary work day had turned into a dude ranch picnic with a crew of elderly ladies. And he was supposed to be patient?

Every day he had taken the truck and driven for miles over the ranch property, until he was acquainted once again with its ridges and valleys, creeks and hay fields. It was a middle-sized ranch, but one that had everything: ranges for all seasons, abundant water and level areas for hay. J.W. had run it well in the years that Will had lived there, but things were different now. It had taken him a while to realize that fact. But because J.W. hadn't taken care of the place for a number of years didn't mean that he, Will Cody, had to step in and take over. The best thing for everyone would be if he sold the ranch. He could give the men some kind of pension, he could help Becky find another job, and he could give his mother the life she deserved.

He didn't know why everyone was against a plan that obviously made sense.

"THAT SON OF YOURS is such a dear," one of the women whispered to Maude. "Has he come back to run the place for you?"

"I hope so," Maude replied, reining in her horse. The Pasos were a big hit, though there weren't enough to go around, of course. But the women had been good about sharing them, arranging to switch horses for the long ride back. Will was limping, though not as much as he had last week. He looked healthier, too. Those dark circles had disappeared from under his eyes. "It all belongs to him now."

She watched as he helped Theresa from her horse and led the animal toward the creek. It was a beautiful day up on the high range, and it had been years since she'd been up here. She took a deep breath and exhaled.

"It's a beautiful place. Do you get up here much?" another one of the women asked.

"No," Maude replied. "I haven't been much for riding these past years, and my brother stopped summering cattle up on this range long ago."

"It would be a wonderful place for a camping trip."

"Yes." There were pine trees and fresh water, a spot not too far from the main house, and not a ride that would be too strenuous for anyone. Food and tents could be brought round by truck, on the back road. She looked around at the others, who appeared to be no worse for wear from the three-hour ride. Of course the cowboys had done most of the work, with the women in the rear making sure no calves wandered off. It had gone surprisingly well, considering the men's shock over the plan originally. "You're right. When shall we do it?"

The other woman smiled. "Why, any time at all, Maude. None of us is going anywhere."

"That's true." She waved Will over, just as Becky appeared with the children.

"Daddy!" Tommy cried.

Theresa turned to Maude. "*Daddy?* What is that all about?"

"Isn't that sweet? The child calls Will that. We don't know why."

"Will's probably the first man the child's seen who hasn't looked like a grandfather," the doctor pointed out. "He may have seen fathers on television."

"He's not even two."

Theresa shrugged. "I've seen stranger things. Your son doesn't seem to mind." The women watched as Will went over and greeted the young woman and her sons. He swung the toddler onto his shoulders and walked over to the cowboys who were taking care of the horses.

"He's grown used to it."

"Well, that's interesting, too," Theresa said. "He and the girl make a nice-looking couple."

"I think so," Maude agreed. "He's going to stay for the summer. I have my fingers crossed that she'll get him to stay permanently. She's a lovely young woman. I couldn't ask for a nicer daughter-in-law."

"A lot can happen in one summer," Theresa assured her friend. "I met and married my Henry in three weeks."

"Really?"

"Oh, yes, indeed. Once you know you've found the right man, why wait?"

"Young people today don't marry like that anymore. They just have sex and maybe live together for a while, then they go their separate ways. I never did understand it myself."

Theresa patted Maude's shoulder. "We're a different generation, Maude. We don't see things the way they do today. Everything's so fast, so busy."

Maude looked around at the rounded foothills at the base of the Rockies. The sun shone brightly in the biggest blue sky she'd ever seen, and a breeze cooled her forehead after she'd removed her hat. "Not here," she said. "Up here everything's the same as it always was."

"And a good thing it is, too," Theresa agreed. They watched as the men followed Will over the ridge. "I guess they've gone to get lunch."

Maude waved at Becky, who had let Peter run after the men. "She works too hard."

"She's young. And she looks happy. Don't worry about her."

"I'll try," Maude said with a sigh. "I want her to stay around for a long, long time."

"YOU'RE RIGHT," Becky said, looking around at the grazing land. "I should have had the cows brought up here early in the summer."

"You can't know everything," Will said, lifting Tommy from his shoulders and setting him down on the blanket spread under a scrub pine. Becky had set up an assortment of simple picnic food for all of the cowhands, and the ladies looked as if they were having a wonderful time. They'd spread out several blankets under nearby trees and were eating the lunch Becky had brought. "You haven't been ranching here long enough."

"Decker suggested it once, but the cattle were doing fine where they were, and I thought it would be too hard to try to herd them up here."

"The lower pastures are getting overgrazed."

"How bad is that?" She didn't want to have done anything wrong, anything that would damage the ranch. She handed the baby a plastic cup of diced fruit and a plastic spoon. He wouldn't use the spoon, but would throw a fit if he didn't have one just like everyone else.

"You have to rest the land once in a while. A lot of ranchers have gone to a four-year rotation program that mimics the way the buffalo used the land."

He sounded more like a professor than a rodeo rider with a killer smile. "How do you know all of this?"

He shrugged. "I read. I have friends around the country who have some pretty big outfits."

"And yet, you never came here."

"I wasn't welcome. I'm sure you've heard the story."

She shook her head. "Just that there was an argument and you left."

He frowned. "That about sums it up. Aren't you going to eat?"

"Sure." She watched as he sat down by Tommy and picked up a thick beef sandwich. So he was going to sit here and eat with her. She could hear Maude's friends now, saying things like, "Look at the young people, don't they look nice together?"

Peter ran over. "Mr. Decker needs another soda pop!"

"Over there." Becky pointed to the red cooler that she'd filled with cold drinks. Peter had managed to escape his mother and eat his lunch with the cowboys. He grabbed a can of root beer and hurried back to the older men who, clustered under the shade of a tree, looked as if they were deliberately avoiding the group of chatting women.

"Doesn't he ride?"

"Peter?" He nodded. "He's only four."

"He's old enough to start," Will said. "Maude's old horse would be good for him. As a place to learn, anyway."

"Maybe." She picked up half a ham sandwich and began to eat. It had been fun to put together the picnic this morning, to have a couple of hours to putter in the kitchen all by herself. Tommy had played on the floor with the pots and pans, while Peter had talked to the dog and colored pictures on a thick pad. She wasn't sure her son was old enough to climb on a horse and take off across the ranch.

"You're frowning," Will said. "Don't you like horses?"

"I'm just thinking that he seems too young to start riding."

"He's not." But Will smiled at her, and the expression softened the harsh lines on his face. He looked younger when he smiled. And sexier, too, which of course wasn't at all the way Becky wanted the man to look. She preferred him to be distant and cold, bossy and aloof. That way she could find it easy to ignore him.

"That's easy for you to say," she quipped, and rolled the wax paper wrapping into a little ball.

"Let me put him up on one of the old mares tomorrow." He pointed to the group of quarter horses tethered under a clump of trees. "See the dun-colored mare? She must be one of the gentlest horses in Montana."

"Yes, she is. Decker always takes her."

"She'd be a good horse to start with."

"I don't have the time to teach Peter to ride."

"I'll do it," he said. "If you let me."

"Why?"

"Every boy should know how to ride."

"Maybe. When they're six." She smiled, knowing she was starting to sound silly and overprotective. Still, she couldn't picture Peter astride a horse all by himself. He'd ridden in front of her for short distances, but she'd had her arms around him and that had given her the feeling that she was still in charge, still capable of preventing injuries.

Tommy stayed close to Will and finished his fruit and pieces of cheese, then Becky handed him a cookie.

"T'anks," he told her, breaking the cookie in half so he could hold a piece in each hand. "See?" He held it up to Will. "Look."

"Looks good," Will agreed, seemingly unaware that there were sticky fingerprints on his short sleeved shirt. He turned back to Becky. "How long were you married?"

The change of subject took her by surprise. "Three years. Just long enough to have Peter and be pregnant with Tommy."

"So you've been a widow a couple of years now."

"That's right."

"What happened? Do you mind my asking?"

"He crashed his truck into a ditch."

"I'm sorry."

"So was I. He was a man who...liked to take chances. Drove too fast, drank too much, partied too hard. I thought he'd settle down when we got married, but I was wrong." She turned away and began to gather up the food and repackage it for the trip home. "I guess we'd better get going. Tommy's going to need a nap soon, and it's a long drive back to the ranch."

"Becky! Will!" Maude called as she hurried toward them. She caught her breath when she came up to the blanket. "Becky, that was lovely. Just the right touch to a wonderful day."

"I'm glad," Becky said, smiling up at her. "Everyone looks like they're having a good time."

"Oh, we all are." She turned to her son. "But I think we'd better start getting back. Decker is going to get the horses ready and lead us down."

He made a move to stand up, but stopped. Tommy was nestled on the blanket next to him, his head on Will's knee, and his eyes were closed. Will looked at Becky. "What do I do now?"

"Don't move," Maude answered. "You don't want to wake the child. Decker will take us back. You can catch up with us."

"I won't be back right away. As long as I'm up here I plan on checking the fence line."

"Then we won't expect you till suppertime." She waved, thanked Becky for lunch again, then rejoined her friends who were gathering by the horses.

Becky looked at her sleeping son. "I can move him."

"Without waking him up?"

"Well," she began, but Peter ran up.

"Mom! Can I go with Mr. Decker?"

"On the horse?"

"I told you," Will said quietly, but Becky ignored him.

"Yeah, Mom. Where else?"

"Don't be fresh," she said, and he immediately looked contrite. "I'm not sure if that's such a good idea."

"Mr. Decker's given me rides before. I know how to sit real still and not bother the horse."

"Oh, you do, huh?"

"Yep." He looked up at her, all earnest blue eyes and golden brown hair. He wasn't a baby anymore, Becky realized. He was growing up and he lived on a ranch and he would want to ride with the men sooner or later, and this was sooner. She looked over toward the men, and Decker caught her eye and gave her the thumbs-up sign. She'd trust the old cowboy with her life, so she turned back to Peter.

"Okay, but be careful and do what Mr. Decker tells you to do."

"I will." He waved at Will then turned around and ran as fast as his little legs would carry him back to the waiting cowboy and dun mare.

"He probably thinks he'd better run away before I change my mind." She sat back on the blanket and continued putting lids on plastic containers of leftover food. She looked over at Tommy. His head on Will's thigh didn't look very comfortable, so she tucked the food into a cardboard box and then scooted over to the sleeping child.

"You don't have to wake him," Will said. "I can sit here for a couple of minutes."

"No, that's okay. You have work to do and so do I." She gently eased her hand under Tommy's head, ignoring the warmth of Will's jean-covered thigh and the embarrassing closeness between the two of them. She cradled the child's head in her hand and moved him so he lay on the blanket. He never opened his eyes, so she covered his shoulders with a dish towel that she'd brought to line a basket of rolls. Will edged away until he was off the blanket, then he stood up.

"I'll be back," he said, before striding off to the group of men, horses and women. Becky packed up the food, dumping the trash into a plastic bag and putting the tin plates into another box she'd brought for dirty dishes. She'd carry everything to the car after Tommy woke up, but for now she'd pack everything up and be prepared to leave. Maybe he would go back to sleep in the car. It was an hour's drive home, a good time for a nap.

When she'd finished that chore, and waved goodbye to Maude, Peter and the rest, Will returned to the shaded blanket and sat down beside her.

"I'll take these to the car for you," he offered, picking up one of the boxes.

"Thanks, but—"

"Stay here with the baby," Will ordered.

Well, that was a good order, Becky thought, smiling to herself. She wouldn't mind sitting under this tree high in the foothills of the Rockies, while a man packed up the station wagon for her. There was a bit of shade and a good breeze, with a view of the ranch valley below that was breathtaking. She should have driven up here more often. If not for moving cattle, then just to sit and enjoy the quiet. But there wasn't time for sitting around, not with all the work there was to do.

Will returned, scooped up the rest of the boxes and plastic bags, and made another trip over the hill to where the car was parked. There were a series of gravel roads

that intersected the ranch, but she hadn't driven on all
of them, at least not enough to know her way around.
That wouldn't matter now, with Will talking about selling. It didn't make sense to sell a place that could be fixed
up. That it was old and needed work only made it more
of a challenge.

Will returned and, instead of expecting her to stand,
sat down on the blanket beside her. He took off his hat,
lay back and closed his eyes.

"I thought you were going to fix fence," Becky said,
keeping her voice low. She sat between the sleeping baby
and the cowboy and fought the urge to take a nap, too.
Just looking at the two of them was making her want to
yawn.

Will kept his eyes closed. "I've been herding women
and cows for hours. The fence can wait a few more minutes."

She knew she should go. If she left now, she could get
a head start on dinner before the others came back. If she
left now, she would miss sitting in one spot for a while
and enjoying the quiet. She leaned back, too, just a little, and rested on her bent arms. That felt so good she
pondered stretching out, too. After all, there was plenty
of room on the blanket to lie down without touching the
man beside her. She shouldn't be the least bit embarrassed, she reminded herself, and scooted down so her
head was next to the baby's. Somewhere overhead a bird
called, and Becky told herself she was just resting, nothing else. What else could she do, she mused, with Tommy
and Will sound asleep? Waking them up would be cruel.
She tucked her arms under her head and closed her eyes.
The last thing she heard was the sound of the wind.

"Becky?"

The voice was low, near her ear. She turned toward it and opened her eyes, only to find her face inches apart from Will's. His eyes were dark; she'd never noticed the thick eyelashes before. She must have fallen asleep, because she couldn't remember where she was or what she was doing.

"You've been sleeping," he supplied, sensing her confusion. "We all have."

Another face came into view, this time the chubby face of Tommy. He smiled, all pink cheeks and happy expression as he leaned over her legs to peer at her. "Mommy! Wake up!"

"Okay," Becky said, trying to do that. She never took naps, but she rarely sat down in the middle of the day either. She struggled to sit up, and Will gave her his hand and helped pull her to a sitting position.

"How long—"

"About thirty minutes." He grinned. "I guess we all needed the rest."

Tommy found a piece of cookie and picked it up from the blanket and put it in his mouth. "Cookies," he said, smiling at them.

"I'll give you another one later," she promised, and turned back to the man beside her. "He likes . . ."

He was too close, and his gaze had dropped to her lips. She hadn't realized that he still held her hand, and when she moved to pull it away he didn't release her. Instead he tugged her ever so gently toward him until their lips were almost touching. He hesitated then, as if thinking it over. And Becky was too surprised to move away. He leaned forward enough to touch her lips with his, a brief exploring kiss that deepened into something stronger. He continued to hold her hand, but otherwise their bodies remained apart. Becky tilted her head, he slanted his lips across hers and kissed her as if he meant it. Becky wanted to lean into him, wanted to curl her fingers into his hair and forget that she worked for him now, that they were not alone, that this wasn't simply a temporary lapse in judgment.

When he was done, he lifted his mouth from hers and looked into her eyes. "Sorry," he said, with little sorrow coloring his voice. "I couldn't resist it."

"Daddy! I wanna see horse," Tommy said, saving Becky from having to come up with a response. She didn't know if she was sorry or not that he'd kissed her. But she couldn't think while he looked at her. Tommy tumbled into Will's lap and threw his arms around the man's neck.

"I'll show you the horse," Will said, "but I'm not your daddy." He put his hat on and looked over at Becky. "Can't you get him to stop calling me that?"

"I've tried. He doesn't seem to understand." She held out her arms. "Come here, Tommy."

"No," the boy said. "No, no, no."

Will chuckled. "I guess we're going to go see the horse." He stood up, swinging the child into his arms at the same time.

"I guess you are," Becky said, wishing her voice didn't sound quite so trembly. She stood up and, as Will and Tommy went to pet the chestnut mare, Becky folded the blanket into a neat square and gathered up the few things that still remained. He'd kissed her, but she wouldn't think about that now.

It was meaningless anyway. Just a little temptation in the middle of a quiet afternoon. That kind of thing wouldn't happen again, she knew. She turned and watched the patient way Will lifted Tommy onto the horse and let him pretend to ride the animal. The cowboy, for all of his faults, was kind to the children.

But that didn't mean their mother had to go around kissing the man. He was another one of those men who couldn't stay long in one place, who had to have the excitement of the rodeo and the adventure of traveling from one place to another. He wasn't for her. She needed a man who would come home for supper each night, who would be right there in the bed with her come sunrise.

Becky waited for Will and her son to quit playing with the horse and start toward her. She would take her son home and stop thinking foolish thoughts. And she would certainly try to forget this had ever happened.

THAT WAS DUMB, Will concluded. He had a lot of time to think about what a dumb stunt he'd pulled, kissing Becky like that. It was just that she'd looked so sweet, napping like that. He'd never seen her totally still before. He hadn't slept long, just dozed for a few minutes. And then he'd become intrigued with watching her until the little boy started to stir.

Then he'd known he should wake her, though he hated to do it. She was a pretty woman. He'd like to know what she'd look like with her hair down and all soft and curling around her face.

He should never have taken her hand. He never should have touched her at all. Will grimaced as he came to yet another section of trampled fence wire. He had brought the necessary supplies to fix fence, but it wasn't a job that anyone really liked to do.

But it had to be done, and the others couldn't be expected to work such long hours. He took a hammer from his pack and fixed the wire, muttering an oath when he hit the edge of his thumb on the second stroke of the hammer. He should never have kissed her.

Or he should never have stopped.

BECKY DROVE DOWN the mountain talking nonstop to her son. "You have to stop calling Will 'Daddy.' He's not your daddy."

Tommy just grinned at her. "I ride horse," he said. "Nice horse."

"Yes, it was a nice horse, but you can't go around calling people daddy. It's embarrassing," she muttered under her breath. She'd seen a couple of the women's faces when they'd heard Tommy holler to Will when they arrived. She hoped Maude had explained that the toddler was a little mixed-up and was no one's love child, least of all Will Cody's.

"You had a daddy, but he went to heaven," Becky tried again, but the toddler bounced in his car seat and pointed toward some cattle. "Cows, Mamma, cows!"

"I know." There was no shortage of cows, even if Will felt they weren't running enough head to make a profit. How on earth was she supposed to know how much stock to run or where to graze them? If Decker or Cal didn't tell her, she wouldn't know. And she couldn't expect the men to know everything about a ranch they hadn't lived on for at least ten years.

From now on, Becky decided, moving slowly along the winding gravel road, she would let Will call the shots around here. It was his ranch; it was time he took care of it. That would leave her time to help Maude with the horses and the entertaining. They would make the most of the SV while they could.

7

"IS THE MOWER GOING to be ready soon?"

Cal looked up from his cup of coffee and blinked at the morning sun shining through the kitchen window of the bunkhouse. "I reckon I don't know."

"Well, when, then?" Will tried to hide his frustration. They were losing valuable time by not getting the hay cut now. The weather was good, hot and dry, and no rain was forecast for the next few days.

"I need a couple of parts. Waiting for them to arrive."

"In town?"

"Yeah. At Barker's. He said he'd call when they came in."

"I'll give them a call and see what the holdup is." Will turned to Decker. "We'll start with the eastern meadow, then move north."

"Who's going to do the driving?"

"I plan to," Will said, watching expressions of relief cross the men's faces. None of the men wanted to admit their eyesight wasn't what it used to be. "I haven't done it in years, but I guess it's still the same."

"I reckon it is," Decker said. "And the baler?"

Will turned to back to Cal. "That's waiting for parts, too?"

"Yep. The forklift is working okay, though."

Which didn't mean anything right now, if the mower couldn't cut the hay into windrows and the baler, which took the windrows and rolled the hay into round bales, wasn't working either. No wonder his uncle hadn't bothered haying. He'd let the cattle survive as best they could on the winter range without feeding them anything. A hell of a way to run a cattle operation, Will fumed.

He poured himself another cup of coffee and walked over to the window to see if Becky was around yet. He'd taken over the morning meetings with the men during the past days. He thought she'd squawk about that, but she hadn't. She'd just looked at him for a long moment as if she couldn't figure out what he was doing, then she'd gone back to washing dishes.

"I don't understand women," Will muttered, then realized too late that he'd spoken out loud.

"No one does," Cal drawled. "It ain't possible."

Will didn't turn away from the window. A truck was coming up the road, which interested him. It was only eight o'clock on a Saturday morning, not a time to be expecting visitors. "Someone's coming."

"Might be one of Maude's friends again," Decker said, walking over to stand beside Will and peer out the window. Cal got up too and tried to look past Will's shoulder.

"Probably Doc Thomas. I had Becky call him for more vaccine."

Decker went back to his coffee. "He's always happy to get a call from the SV. I think he goes to bed nights prayin' for an excuse to get out here."

Will turned from the window. "Decker, what the hell are you talking about?"

"Doc Thomas. He's a little older than you, never married. He has a little place in town."

"So?"

"So," Decker drawled, looking as if he wanted to smile. "So maybe he likes to visit ranches where there's a pretty blond single lady who smiles real nice and ain't afraid of a little cow manure."

"Becky."

"Well, you have to wonder why no red-blooded man has taken her out of here."

"She's a widow."

"For a couple of years. She's young, and she warn't married long. Plenty of time to have more little ones and set up housekeeping again."

"Does she like this guy?"

Decker shrugged. "Hard to tell. But she might like him more now, with you talking about selling out and her needing a home. She might be looking to the future more than she used to."

Will turned back to the window and frowned. A shiny green truck rolled into the yard by the house and came to a stop. A tall heavy man stepped out, tucked in his shirt and slicked back his hair with the palm of his hand before putting on his hat. He looked for all the world like a man going courting. He looked like an idiot. In fact, he was an idiot if he thought he had a chance with Becky. Will headed toward the door. He intended to find out exactly what was on the veterinarian's mind.

"That was mighty interesting," Decker said to the others after Will hurried out the door. The men crowded around the windows and watched the young man walk past the barns and outbuildings toward the main house.

"You bet," Cal agreed. "This is all gonna get pretty good now."

"Just like Maude said," Decker added.

"Maude?" Oatey glanced his way. "Does that old gal have something to do with this?"

"Well, she didn't call the vet, that's for sure," Decker replied. "But she said the two of them—our Miss Becky and Will—are perfect for each other."

They all nodded their agreement.

Oatey looked doubtful. "Will doesn't think so, I'll bet."

"That boy's got a long way to go," Decker warned. "He'll be a hard one to pin down, I told Maude. She thinks it's only a matter of time. If they spend enough time together, that is."

"Time together," Cal repeated. "I reckon that could be arranged."

Malone scratched his head. "How do we do that?"

"We've got to leave them alone. Things always happen when a young couple spends time alone."

They nodded at Decker's wisdom. They always nodded at Decker's wisdom.

"You want one of us to go out there and cut Doc Thomas out of the herd?"

Decker shook his head. "Nope. The boss needs a kick in the butt, and the vet might be just the one to do it." He turned from the window as Will disappeared from view. "Let's make ourselves another pot of coffee and leave the young people to sort this one out."

Cal nodded. "We'll leave 'em alone then, starting now."

"Damn right," Malone agreed, and Oatey, not to be left out, yawned and nodded his agreement.

BECKY DIDN'T EXPECT to see Mike Thomas at the back door, but she waved him in. "You're around pretty early, especially on a Saturday," she said, automatically pouring him a cup of coffee. He was a nice-looking man, with a square face and light brown hair. His eyes were kind, and he tended to be shy. She'd always felt bad about the twice he'd asked her out. It was hard to be interested in dating when you were so tired you wanted to cry.

"I brought extra vaccine," he explained, stepping carefully into the kitchen. Lady trotted in and growled at him.

"Australian shepherd," the vet said. "Nice breed for herding cattle." He stood still and let the dog sniff his hand before he moved into the kitchen. "When did you get her?"

Becky handed him the coffee. "She's not mine. Maude's son is here for a while and she belongs to him, though lately she's so attached to Peter I think she's forgotten who she belongs to." The dog turned away and left the room, heading toward the den where Peter was watching cartoons on television.

"Thanks." He sat down at the kitchen table and took a sip. "I heard Maude's son came home to sell the ranch."

"That's what he says, though Maude's hoping he'll change his mind."

"Well, if he's anything like his uncle, he won't," the vet declared.

"I'm afraid I don't understand your meaning," Will said, walking into the room. Becky looked up, realizing that Will must have been on the porch long enough to have overheard.

"We were just talking—" she started to say, but Mike had turned toward Will and stood up. The vet stuck out his hand.

"You must be Maude's son. I'm Mike Thomas, local horse doctor."

Will had no choice but to shake the man's hand. "Will Cody. Glad to meet you."

He didn't sound glad, Becky noted. In fact, he sounded like he'd had a rough morning and wanted to take it out on someone. Too bad the shy veterinarian was the first man who got in his way. "Want coffee?"

"Sure."

Lady stuck her head in the kitchen, saw Will and turned around without greeting him. *Oh, it's only you,* seemed to be her expression, and Becky smiled as she poured the coffee. Maude was still asleep, and Tommy, tolerating his playpen, was watching cartoons in the den with Peter. Becky put the mug on the table in front of Will and turned to the vet.

"I'll bet you've come to see the Pasos."

"Yes, that and to see if you needed any medical supplies. And I also wanted to ask you—"

"Mike," Will interjected, cutting off the man's words. "What do you know about these Spanish horses my mother has bought?"

Mike turned away from Becky. "Well, they're supposed to be fine riding horses, from what I've heard."

"I'd like you to look them over, if you don't mind."

"Well," the vet hesitated, looking at Becky who was leaning against the counter watching the men. She smiled, and he said, "Sure, I'll be glad to have a quick look. I'm due over at the Jeffersons', but it's not an emergency."

"Great," Will said, standing up. "Let's go."

"Uh, fine." He put down his coffee and turned to Becky. "Are you coming?"

"I can't leave the boys alone," she said.

"Then I'll stop in on my way out."

"Come on, Doc," Will urged, slapping his hat on his head. "We're wasting time."

Wasting time? Becky had seen him make a cup of coffee last half an hour while he doodled in his account books or talked about cattle with Decker. He wasn't a morning person by any stretch of the imagination, yet here he was acting like he had as much energy as Tommy.

"See ya," Mike said, casting a wistful look her way. She watched the men leave and heard the screen door shut. Mike Thomas was going to ask her out again. Maybe it would be good to go out with the man. Maybe she needed to get out, date again, see someone other than Will Cody. Perhaps going out with Doc Thomas would dilute the attraction she had to the rodeo rider. Mike was a nice man, even though his conversation tended to be mostly about bovine diseases. He loved cattle and he certainly seemed to enjoy working in this part of Montana. She would say yes. Unless she couldn't find a sitter or one of the boys took sick or Maude needed her for something that no one else could do. She would say yes to Mike and she would put Will Cody and his bone-melting kiss right out of her mind once and for all.

"WELL, I DON'T THINK it's right that you should be baby-sitting, that's all," Will grumbled. He'd had to watch Becky climb into the vet's truck and head for town. She'd mentioned dinner and the early movie at the Ortheum, Dry Gulch's new twin cinema. She'd worn a pretty dress, looped her long hair at the nape of her neck and she'd had lipstick on. Lipstick! For the vet.

"I don't mind." Maude reached over and gave Tommy another cracker. "I can pretend they're my grandchildren."

"That's ridiculous."

"At this rate I'll never have any from you, so why not have fun with Becky's boys?" She tickled Tommy's chin and made him smile.

"You don't know that I won't have children. I've never said that." The little boy broke the cracker in half and stretched his hand toward Will.

"Daddy? 'Racker, okay?"

Will took the soggy piece of cracker and pretended to eat it. "Thanks, kid."

Maude gave Will a withering look. "As if your lifestyle would be good for raising a family!"

"I've made a lot of money working the rodeo," he said, defending himself.

"Money isn't everything," she sniffed. "Whatever happened to love and family and settling down?"

He sighed and picked up his glass of iced tea. "I will, when I'm older."

"You're old enough now, with a busted knee and a hurt back."

"Don't remind me. It's getting better."

"And you'll get hurt all over again, the minute you start up riding broncs and bulls again. Don't think you're fooling me."

"I don't," he said, but he did. He was fooling himself, too, thinking that he could go back to he rodeo. The doctor had warned him he'd be crippled permanently if he kept working. Trouble was, he didn't know anything else. Ranching didn't count. He sure as hell wasn't going to stay here. Maybe he'd buy a bigger place after the SV was sold. That was a possibility, too. But he didn't want to have employees, he didn't want to have to worry about bank loans and frozen calves born too soon, or horses that got sick for mysterious reasons and fence that always needed fixing.

He wondered what he did want. And he knew.

"Let's go to town," he said, giving his mother what he hoped was a charming, irresistible smile.

"You can. I can't." She pointed to Tommy. "I'm baby-sitting, remember?"

"We'll all go. We'll take the kids and get some ice-cream cones. They still have ice cream at the Dairy Freeze, don't they?"

She gave him an odd look, like he'd lost his mind. "Well, yes, I guess so, but—"

"You like ice cream, Tommy?"

The little boy smiled. "I like Daddy. Ice cream?"

"Good. It's two against one." He stood up. "I'll take a quick shower and clean up, then we'll take the wagon and go to town. Is the car seat still in there?"

"It should be."

"Fine. Ice cream it is, then." He hurried upstairs to clean up before Maude could change her mind. Becky wasn't the only person who could go to town on a Saturday night.

"WE CAN'T SPOIL Becky's evening," Maude said, coming to a halt on the sidewalk.

"We're not spoiling anything," Will lied. He fully intended to interrupt any romantic inclinations that the veterinarian had toward Becky. He looked up at the marquee. "She's seeing one movie, we'll be seeing another."

"Oh, boy!" Peter grinned and hurried to the poster of a three-headed monster.

"That looks scary," Maude protested.

"It's supposed to be funny. It's a Disney picture. Rated PG." And it got out three minutes before the romantic comedy next door, the one he was sure Becky and the horny doctor were seeing.

"Popcorn," Tommy said, pointing to the window where a large machine popped corn. Will tightened his grip on the boy before he could lunge out of his arms. "Does this kid ever stop eating?"

"He's a growing boy."

Will stepped up to the window and bought the tickets. "One adult, one senior citizen and two children," he told the teenager at the cash register.

"I hate being called that," Maude grumbled.

"What?" He lifted Tommy from his shoulders and realized they hadn't brought extra diapers. Then he tucked him under his arm and corralled Pete, who had wandered down the sidewalk in search of pennies.

"Senior citi— Where are you going?"

"Herding calves," he muttered, guiding them all inside the theater. Originally one screen, the folks who owned it had split it into two smaller theaters. The one showing the PG-rated monster movie was packed with kids. Big kids, little kids and noisy kids, all eating candy or popcorn. Most were throwing candy or popcorn at each other.

"I'm not sure this is such a good idea," Maude said, rejecting one seat because it was covered with something sticky.

"Over here," Will said, finding four seats on the side. It was a damn good idea to be in the same place as Becky and her date. The guy was new in town. He could be some kind of sex pervert.

Peter looked around, clearly impressed by the activity. "Can we have popcorn?"

"Popcorn! Popcorn!" Tommy bounced up and down in his seat, then climbed on Will's lap and waited for the popcorn to appear.

"Sure." He gave the baby to Maude and took Peter with him to buy soda pop, a big container of buttered popcorn and a fistful of overpriced candy bars. They would have fun. They would see their mother afterward, and she wouldn't be able to resist going home with them instead of the mysterious doctor. He was doing her a favor.

Will started to doubt himself fifteen minutes into the movie. Cartoon monsters were still monsters, and Tommy started to whimper whenever the purple one with the big teeth appeared on the screen. The child sat on Will's lap, his arms wrapped around the man's neck. Peter was entranced, ate enough popcorn to feed a yearling calf for a year, and belched his way through a container of root beer that was supposed to be a medium and looked like half a gallon.

It took a few minutes to get out of the theater when the movie had ended. Tommy cried for his mother and Peter had to go to the bathroom, so Will took him and left Tommy screaming "Daddy, Daddy!" at the top of his lungs.

When he returned to the lobby with Peter, Becky and her square-faced date were talking to Maude. Tommy was in Becky's arms and the doc had the nerve to smile at the child as if he liked kids.

Tommy screamed. Will hid a smile. The doc looked a little like the nasty big-headed monster that ate all the little boys' licorice sticks. "Not my daddy," the little boy hollered. "Go away!"

The vet backed up a step. "I don't think I've met your younger son," he said to Becky.

"He's overexcited," Maude said.

"He must be tired." Becky patted Tommy's back and said something soothing as Peter and Will joined them.

"Hey," Will said, as Tommy lifted his tearstained face from his mother's shoulders and looked at the cowboy. Will felt his heart drop. He held out his arms and took the boy from Becky. Poor Tommy looked as if he'd had enough excitement for one day. "He had fun at the movie, for most of the time," he tried to explain. Becky looked as if she didn't believe him.

"I didn't know you were coming to the show," she said.

"Hi, Doc," Will said, nodding toward the now confused looking man. Good. Let him see that dating Becky wasn't going to be as easy as he thought. "How was the movie?"

"Fine," the man said, taking Becky's elbow. "We were just going out for a drink. Too bad you can't join us."

"Yeah. Too bad." The doc didn't sound sorry, Will noticed. Relieved was more like it.

"Mom?" Peter looked up at her. "When are you coming home?"

"Soon," she promised, giving Peter a kiss. "You go home and go to bed. I won't be much longer."

"Take your time," Maude insisted. "They'll go right to sleep."

"Mama?" Tommy reached out one hand, while his head rested on Will's shoulder.

"Night-night," Becky said. The vet shifted impatiently.

"We really should—"

"Say good-night to Mommy," Will interjected. "She'll be home soon."

"'Night, Mommy." Tommy, his face sticky with dried chocolate, yawned.

Becky looked torn, as if she wanted to go home with the children, yet couldn't get rid of her date. Good, Will thought. She needed to be home anyway.

"Let's go," Will said, taking Peter's hand. "I'll tell you a story about a rodeo clown before you go to sleep."

"Take your time," Maude repeated, saying good-night to the couple.

"I'll be home soon," Becky promised.

Will tried to look as if he didn't care. "No hurry." He led his little family down the sidewalk and around the corner to where he'd parked the station wagon. That had gone well. Nothing romantic was going to happen between Becky and the doc while she had visions of her sons looking as if they needed her at home. He got the kids settled inside the wagon, then began the long ride back to the ranch.

"Are you proud of yourself?" Maude whispered.

"Proud of what?" Will kept his voice carefully casual.

"That little performance," Maude said. "Now I understand why you *had* to go to town tonight—"

"It's Saturday," he interjected. "Going to town on a Saturday night is not exactly an original idea."

"And why you *had* to go to the movies," she finished, ignoring his words. "You wanted to ruin that girl's evening."

Will looked in the rearview mirror and saw that both boys were asleep. "Ruin it? Do you think so?"

"Becky never gets to go out and have a nice time. And there we were, following her around with her children." Maude sighed. "I hope she'll forgive me."

"Forgive you? It was all my idea." And it was a good one, too. "Besides, the kids had fun. And just how much do you know about that vet, anyway?"

"His father's a minister down in Bozeman. He's highly thought of around here. He's done a good job."

"And he's looking for a wife, too, I'll bet."

"Well, not everyone is like you," Maude commented. "Most men want to find a good woman and settle down."

"Yeah, well, I'm not most men." What he wanted to do was take Becky into the barn or the stable or the nearest bedroom and make love to her. Most men would want the same thing, but he didn't point that out to his mother. "And the doctor there might not want to get married either, especially to a woman with two children."

Maude sighed. "That's the trouble. I never got a chance to marry again after your father died, and I always regretted it. I hate to see Becky stuck on the ranch, with only a few old people for company. She needs to be around people her own age."

"She could get a job in town when the ranch is sold. Or she could move to a town like Bozeman." Will realized he didn't like that idea much himself.

"I thought we weren't going to talk about selling out, at least not for a while."

He shrugged. "I still think it's a good idea."

"I don't."

"It's for your own good."

"I should know what's for my own good," Maude declared. "I'm older than you, and wiser. Just because you want something your way doesn't mean you're going to get it, young man."

Will smiled over at her. "Yes, ma'am, I'll keep that in mind."

"And leave Becky alone, unless you're planning to stick around." She closed her eyes and leaned her head back, ending the conversation. Will frowned into the darkness as the miles sped by. They would be home in a little while, and he found himself looking forward to turning down that road. For the first time in his life he felt he had a place to come home to.

A dangerous thought, he realized, gripping the steering wheel. He wasn't the kind of man to stay in one place. He was used to traveling, to being on his own. He was accustomed to living a life that didn't depend on the weather and the price of beef and the opinions of women. It was a good life, but somehow he had the unsettling feeling that it was all going to change. And there wouldn't be a damn thing he could do about it.

SHE SHOULD HAVE expected Will to be awake still when she got home. After all, it wasn't even eleven o'clock. It just felt later, especially since she'd been up since five, but the living-room lights were on. Becky opened the back door quietly as Mike drove away, and walked swiftly through the kitchen and up the back stairs to her room.

She didn't want to see anyone, least of all Will Cody. She didn't know what he'd been doing, taking her kids to the movies and acting as if he were having a good time. Tommy Lee had snuggled into the cowboy's arms and called him Daddy and later her date had asked an awful lot of questions about Maude's son and his plans for the future.

It had been embarrassing. She hurried to the boys' room, peeked to make sure they were all right, then left their room to go to her own.

"So, you're home," Will said. He leaned against the doorjamb, effectively blocking the door to her bedroom. The hall was dark, except for the small glow of a night-light by the stairs. "You're home early."

"I'm tired."

"Or he's as boring as he looks," Will muttered, reaching for her doorknob. He swung her door open. "There you go. All yours."

"Thanks." She waited for him to move away, but he didn't. "That was nice of you to take the kids to town."

He shrugged. "They're good kids."

"Yes."

"I might've fed 'em too much."

"That's okay." She waited once again for him to move out of the way.

"What about you?"

"What about me?"

"Did the vet feed you?"

"Yes."

"Did you have a good time?" Becky made a move to go to her room, but he shifted his body slightly to block her. "You didn't answer my question."

"Yes, I had a good time," she replied. She didn't want to stand there in the dark hallway and banter with Will. She felt sad and vulnerable and very much alone tonight, and she didn't want to stand in the hall and tell Will Cody—especially Will Cody—that Mike Thomas had kissed her and it had been a kiss devoid of any passion. At least on her part.

Which was disappointing, because after kissing Will a few days ago, she would have figured she was desperate for a little passion.

"Did he kiss you?"

Becky looked up at him, wondering if he could now read her mind. "That's none of your business."

"Did he kiss you like this?" He bent down and brushed his lips against hers for a sweet, brief moment. Then Will looked at her, and when she didn't answer, he tried again. "Or was it more like this?"

This time he took longer, applied more pressure, tempted her to open her lips with the teasing touch of his tongue. Becky tried not to react, but she touched his forearms in an instinctive need to hold on.

When he lifted his mouth from hers, he didn't move. "Well?"

"I think you'd better—"

"You don't look like a woman who's been kissed," he murmured, touching her cheek with his palm. "At least, not when you came home."

"It's none of your—"

"So he didn't kiss you like this, either," he said, ignoring her feeble protests and taking possession of her lips again. This time his arms went around her. This time her hands crept up to his shoulders. She parted her lips, he took her mouth with his tongue and kissed for long, heated moments until Becky wondered if her knees would hold her. His body was hot and hard, his cotton shirt soft under her fingertips. She touched a triangle of warm skin above the unbuttoned collar of his shirt and wished, for the briefest second, that she could touch more of him. Her body was warm where it was pressed against his, and his mouth tempted her to lose all reason and forget herself.

He ended the kiss and took a deep breath, looking shaken.

"Are you finished?" she managed to say, lifting her chin and taking a step backward, out of his arms. Out of danger. She wouldn't give him the satisfaction of knowing how he'd affected her.

He smiled, and she knew she hadn't fooled him at all. "Now you've been kissed, Miss Becky."

"Am I supposed to say thank-you?"

Will shook his head. "You're supposed to go into that room and shut your door, before we forget where we are."

"And *who* we are," she reminded him. "I'm not one of your rodeo one-night stands."

"Which makes you much more dangerous," he muttered, and backed away from her door. Becky went inside and shut the door behind her. God help her, she wanted to invite him in. She wanted to be held, and she wanted to be loved. And she didn't want to be alone anymore. But Will Cody was not the man for her, and the sooner she could leave the SV the better. There was no sense fooling herself any longer. This wasn't really her home, and the whims of a cowboy could change everything.

8

"YOU SHOULD'VE seen it," Maude said, handing Decker a mug of coffee. They leaned on the fence and looked at the Pasos cavorting in the small pasture. "He was jealous last night. I know he was."

"Will was jealous of the vet?" Decker grinned. "That's goldarn funny, Maudie."

"When he found out Becky was going on a date, he dragged us all to town and to the movies, too, where he had it all figured to just happen to run into Becky and the doc. Acted real casual, too, like he took kids to the movies every Saturday night of his life."

Decker didn't look as if he believed one word she said. "What did Becky do?"

"Well, she wanted to be with those kids, naturally. Which was what my silly son was counting on. But she couldn't be rude to the doc, either, so they went off to get a drink and we came home." Maude surveyed the horses. They were beautiful. and next year there would be foals. And the year after that, too. Everything was going so well now. It made her smile just to think about it all.

Decker gazed at her as if he still didn't believe what she was describing. "And Will? He came home too?"

"Oh, yes, and was he ever pleased with himself! I gave him a piece of my mind on the way home, just so he wouldn't know how tickled I was."

"A smoke screen."

"Yep. He was *jealous*, Decker. From his hat right down to his boots, pure jealous. It was a sight to see, all right." She adjusted her hat against the glare of the sun. "Going to be another hot one today," she muttered. "I don't know what happened after I went to bed, but I made sure to go right upstairs. I can see the road from up there anyway, and it wasn't an hour and a half before Becky came home."

The cowboy grinned. "Must've been a quick drink."

Maude nodded. "She must have hightailed it back to the ranch pretty quick. I feel kinda bad, like I spoiled her evening."

"I wouldn't worry about that, Maude. You've got what they call the 'big picture' in mind," Decker agreed, eyeing his boss.

"That's right, I do. I want her to stay and Will to stay and I want grandchildren. I want this ranch to stay in the family, like it's supposed to. And if Will falls for Becky, then everything will fall into place."

"You're an optimistic woman, Maude."

She shook her head. "I'm a practical woman, Deck. I know what has to be done, and the next step is for Will and Becky to, um, make love."

The old cowboy scratched his head and replaced his hat. "I don't know how the hell you're going to figure that one out. That stuff is sure tricky. In my day, things were simpler."

Maude smiled. "We just need to keep them together. He's a hot-blooded man, and she's a woman who's been alone a long time. Things will take care of themselves."

Decker nodded. "All right. I'll tell the rest of the men. They're already laughin' about the way Will moons around over that young woman."

"Good." Maude sighed with contentment and watched her beautiful horses. "I've got too much at stake to let it all disappear now."

"We all do," Decker reminded her. "Every single one of us is out of a home if Will sells this place."

"I know." Maude sighed. "I'm doing my best, but that boy is sure stubborn. He won't see what's good for him, not when it's right under his nose."

"He'll come around," Decker promised. "The boys and I will help."

Maude nodded, hoping she looked more confident than she felt. A jealous cowboy was nothing new, but one who would settle down and marry a widow with a couple of kids? Now *that* was going to take a miracle.

"MAUDE, I'VE DECIDED to start looking for another job," Becky said. She'd waited until after lunch, when Tommy was with Oatey having a rest and she and Maude were alone in the kitchen. Peter was helping Decker with the horses, and she and Maude were trying to cook a few meals ahead. During the haying they would need more food and have less time to cook it.

"For heaven's sake. Why?" Maude, taking a pan of hard-boiled eggs from the stove, stopped and turned around. Her expression made Becky feel terrible.

"Be careful you don't burn yourself," she said, turning on the cold water faucet as Maude placed the pan in the sink and poured off the boiling water.

"I don't know why we're going to all this trouble for deviled eggs anyway," Maude grumbled.

"They're Decker's favorite. I promised." She left the eggs in the cold water to cool for peeling and went over to the stove to stir the lasagna noodles.

"You can't leave," Maude said, following her. "Just what exactly brought this on?"

"I just think it's time," Becky said, pretending to be engrossed in the pan of boiling pasta. She couldn't say *I'm trying to avoid your sexy son.*

"I'm not letting Will sell the ranch, if that's what you have on your mind," the old woman declared. "We're still going to raise horses and the Not Dead Yet Club is going to pay to ride them. I was talking to a man from Silver Adventures the other day and he's even—"

"Maude, I can't." Her adventures, silver or any other color, were over. It was time she stopped pinning her hopes on breeding horses and the dreams of a very kind but unrealistic employer. The timer went off, announcing the noodles were cooked, so Becky turned the stove off. "Would you take the eggs out of the sink?"

"You want me to leave them in the pan?"

"Sure. I just need the sink free for the colander." It took a few minutes to drain and rinse the noodles, and by the time the job was done Becky's face was flushed and perspiration dotted her forehead. A hot July afternoon wasn't the best time to be cooking, but she didn't have any other free time today, and the job had to be done. According to Decker, the haying would begin soon.

Maude fussed nearby. "I just don't understand," she muttered, watching Becky run cold water over the lasagna noodles.

"This stops them from cooking."

"Not that. Why you think you have to find another job."

"Because you and I both know that everything around here is going to change, whether you like it or not. You can't stop your son from selling this ranch, and you can't blame him for wanting you to move near him."

"*He* should be moving near me," she sniffed. "Everything would be perfect if he'd show some sense."

"He is," Becky said, turning to her friend. "He's trying to do what's best for you, no matter how much you don't think he's doing the right thing. We need help with this place and you and I have to admit it."

"At last," Will said, stepping into the kitchen. "Someone is making sense."

Becky didn't turn around to look at him. She wiped her brow with her sleeve and started opening jars of spaghetti sauce.

"Becky's leaving," Maude told him. "I expect you to do something to change her mind. I'm going to take my nap." She gave her son a withering look as she passed him on her way out of the room. "Do something intelligent, like make her understand she has a job here."

Becky winced. She didn't need Will Cody to talk her into staying, especially after last night.

Will shrugged. "I came in to tell you that your son is going to have a riding lesson. Do you want to watch?"

"Yes. No." She finally looked up at him and hoped she wouldn't blush. She was too old to blush because a cowboy had kissed her. "I don't know."

He tilted his hat from his forehead and frowned at her. "You're not leaving because of what happened last night, are you?"

"Of course not."

"Well, good. Because it's going to happen again." His eyes twinkled with mischief.

"No, it's not," Becky said, but she smiled. She could take his teasing; she couldn't take his lovemaking.

"I guess," he drawled, stepping closer, "that's a matter of opinion. You coming outside or not?"

"Okay, but just for a few minutes. Until I see what you and Peter have cooked up." She untied her apron and tossed it on a chair. "I'm getting food ready for the haying."

"Maude's not having another one of her parties, is she?"

"Well . . ."

He put his hand up. "Don't tell me. I'm sure I'll hear about it soon enough."

Becky grabbed her hat from its hook on the porch and went outside into the bright summer sun. It was hot, with a breeze blowing that did little to cool the air. When they reached the corral, Becky saw her son standing with Decker beside a little mare. He waved when he saw her, and Decker's face broke into a grin.

"Well, well," the old man said. "I see we've got an audience, boy."

Peter didn't leave the horse's side, as if he was afraid that if he did, his mother wouldn't let him return. "Hey, Mom," he called. "I'm gonna be a cowboy!"

"Tell me he's going to be okay." She didn't want to be nervous; she knew better. But he was just a baby, too young to control a huge animal like a horse.

Will gave her a pat on the back. "Look, he'll be fine. He's four, so it's high time he learned about horses."

"No rodeo tricks, okay?"

"Lady, you have one hell of an imagination," he said with a sigh. "We're going to walk that mare around and teach the kid how to behave on a horse." He dropped his hand from her shoulder and walked toward the boy.

"Be careful," Becky urged one last time, but Will turned around and smiled at her.

"Be quiet," he said.

"Okay." She tried to smile, but it wasn't easy. She stayed on the other side of the fence and watched as Will and Peter led the horse into the small riding corral on the east side of the horse barn. With her heart in her throat, she watched Will boost the child onto the back of the horse and walk beside him around the corral. Peter's expression was a combination of excitement and concentration, but he dared to smile at his mother as he passed her.

He looked like his father at that moment, in the days before the marriage had soured and Jack had refused to grow up and take care of his family. Before things had changed, and she'd realized she'd married someone who didn't want anything to do with his family or his responsibilities. He wanted all the good times and none of the hard times that came with raising kids and earning a living.

It had been up to her then and it was up to her now. Which was why she needed to start looking for another job. Will Cody might give his mother another month or two on the ranch, but come fall and the calves gone to market, it would be over.

She waved to Peter again, and her heart burst with pride. He needed a father to do these things, and maybe she ought to think about finding him one of those, too. She looked at the handsome cowboy who rode beside her child. He was a good man, but not her type. He was another wild one, with his eye on the horizon all the time. They might be attracted physically, but she'd be in trouble if she let it go any further than that.

Becky waved once more and returned to her kitchen. Peter was in good hands, and there was lasagna to assemble. She didn't need to stand around and gawk at Will Cody for the rest of the afternoon. She had better things to do, such as tell herself to get a grip and start acting her age.

THEY TOOK TURNS driving the mower, until Will realized that Decker's eyesight wasn't that good, Cal had trouble with gauging distance and Oatey just plain hated the equipment. Malone was the only one, other than Becky, who could cut a straight swath through the field without wrecking something. Oatey had returned to where he was happiest, with the children. It had only taken four days to get the part they needed, and Will had woken each morning glad to see the sun shining. Rain would be the last thing they needed. He wanted to cut as much as possible and show prospective buyers that the ranch could support its cattle with its own winter feed.

Oddly enough, there had been no more contact from the three people interested, but maybe that was typical in the real estate business. Becky hadn't made any more noise about leaving and Maude spent a lot of time on the phone planning things he knew he wouldn't like. Will wiped the sweat from his brow and turned off the engine as Maude drove up with Becky.

"Dinner!" the younger woman called, hopping out of the old truck. He didn't know where she got her energy. He'd taken over planning the day's work with the men, but Becky was still up early, taking care of her kids and cooking breakfast. It seemed as if she was always in the kitchen or with Maude taking care of those fancy horses. Will planned to keep the stallion and maybe a mare or two and take them back to his place. That damn horse was like riding a Cadillac.

"Where's Malone?"

"Gone to get something from town, I think," Maude said. "Here, Becky," she said, turning to the woman.

"Take this to Will while I go back for some more ice. I plumb forgot the lemonade."

"That's okay," Will said. "I can drink water."

"I only brought one jug. I'll have to go back and get the big cooler." Maude fanned herself. "The heat must be making me forgetful."

"Then let someone else come out here from now on." He walked over to the tree where the women had set up lunch. "That's what we have help for."

"I like the drive," his mother insisted. "And the men are busy."

"With what?" It seemed like he and Becky were the only ones putting in a full day's work lately.

"I'm planning a camping trip."

"Not during haying season you're not."

"When you're finished, then. Next week."

He shook his head. "I'm not taking your club of old ladies camping. Someone will get hurt and sue the pants off us."

"I talked to a lawyer. There are ways around that," Maude insisted. He didn't look at his mother, though, because Becky had taken off her hat and was fanning herself as she sat on the picnic blanket. The outline of her breasts was obvious underneath the faded man's shirt.

"The same lawyer who's been calling me?"

"Yes. You really should make an appointment with him, Will. There are things you should—"

"Later," he said, watching Becky pick up a handful of grapes. She was oblivious to him as she popped one after another into her mouth and chewed delicately. "I don't have time to go to town."

Maude sighed. "Well, have it your way, then." She went over to the truck and got in behind the steering wheel. "I'll be back with water and lemonade in a few minutes."

"Yeah," he said, not paying her the least bit of atten- tion. He turned back to Becky and sat down across from her on the blanket.

"Want a sandwich?" she asked. The top two buttons on her shirt were unfastened, giving him a glimpse of collarbone and soft skin. Will eyed that intriguing V, then noticed that Becky was holding out a sandwich.

"Thanks." He took it, realizing that the two of them were alone for the first time since Saturday night. Four days, and he hadn't forgotten how it felt to kiss her. He planned to do it again, but she had a knack for avoiding him. Either that, or there were too damn many people running around the ranch.

"Nice day," she said, looking past him to where the hay he had cut lay piled in thick rows, and in the distance were the foothills of the Rockies, the mountains rising far in the distance. Will took a deep breath and leaned against the tree. There was some satisfaction in putting up hay. More than he remembered. The thick rows would be formed into rolls, then lined up together like long cinnamon rolls. In the winter, one of the men would put the forklift attachment onto a tractor and move each roll where it was needed. The cows, their breath frosty on dark winter mornings, would gather round to feed.

"You're not still thinking about leaving, are you?"

"If you're thinking about selling," was her reply.

"I don't have much choice," he said, hoping he could make her understand. "This place doesn't make any money. It's a losing proposition."

"You couldn't figure out how to make it work?"

"I doubt it."

"Have you even tried?" She poured them cups of water and handed him one. "You've said yourself that your uncle wasn't running enough cattle. And he hadn't bothered with the haying much, either. Maude wants to charge people for riding around the ranch, which might bring in some cash in the summer until the fall sale of the calves. If you were here, we could breed the two-year-old heifers and get through calving season. And some of the neighbors have gone from cow-calf operations to fattening yearlings, which has—"

"Whoa." He put up his hand. "You're forgetting something, honey."

"Honey?" She frowned at him.

He wondered once again what it would be like to unbraid that hair and let it fall over her shoulders. It was a shade lighter than the golden color of the distant hay. "Just a figure of speech." He tore his gaze from her hair to look into those blue eyes. "And I have no interest in making this ranch work, except for those things that will get a better price for it."

"Because you hated your uncle?" She didn't wait for a reply. "When are you going to get over that? You own a piece of one of the most beautiful places in the world, and you act like it's a *problem*. What on earth is the matter with you?"

Well, for one thing, he had a tightening in his groin that had nothing to do with owning part of Montana. Will didn't think Becky would appreciate knowing that fact, though. "There's nothing the matter with me," he said, sounding as if he was lying. Which he was, of course.

"Sure there is," Becky insisted. "I can see why you'd want your mother to move to some nice little apartment in Billings, *if* she was unhappy here. But she's not unhappy—just the opposite, in fact—and yet you keep wanting to move her away."

"And I'm supposed to stay," he said. "I'm supposed to give up a career that makes a lot of money—"

"That knee of yours isn't going to hold up much longer, is it? And you've hurt your back, too. Sometimes you hold yourself like you can barely move and—"

"Be quiet, Becky."

"Why? Because you don't want to hear the truth? You have a *home* here, which is something most people would give their right arm to have. And all you want to do is get rid of it."

"What about you, Becky? Is that what you want, a home like this?" He didn't mean to sound harsh, and he was surprised and a little ashamed when her eyes suddenly filled with tears.

"Of course," she whispered. "Homes aren't easy to come by, you know."

"Tell me about your husband."

She dropped her gaze and started to pick up the lunch leftovers and pack them into little plastic containers. "What do you want to know?"

"Why didn't he give you a home?"

"Things didn't work out that way. We never stayed in one place long enough." She glanced up at him, tried to smile, but failed. "He was always promising that he would find a place of our own, though, but he never did."

"What was his name?"

"Jack."

"And you were happy?"

"For a while. Until Peter came and I wanted to settle down and not live in a trailer anymore. Jack didn't like to stay put. He took cowboy jobs here and there, drifting where the mood took him. He loved to have a good time, which is what killed him." She looked up at Will then. "He'd been drinking and crashed the truck on the way home from the Big Sky Saloon. Luckily no one else was hurt, but he died a couple of days later from head injuries."

"I'm sorry."

"I'd been working part-time for Maude, doing some cooking and cleaning. After the accident, she took me in. I didn't—don't—have any family left, and Jack's folks were gone, too. Maude said she understood what it was like to be alone, with a child. She paid the hospital bills and the funeral expenses. But I've paid her back," she told him. "Every dime."

"That couldn't have been very long ago," he said. "Tommy—"

"Wasn't even born yet. I didn't know I was pregnant until a few months after the accident." She let him take her hand. He looked at her and wondered if she even realized she was holding on to him.

"No wonder you care so much about my mother."

Becky nodded. "She's been a good friend."

"Look," he said, choosing his words carefully. "If I promise to do my best to not hurt her in any way, can we declare a truce?"

"You never answered my question," she said, pulling her hand away with a gentle tug. "What's so bad about staying here?"

"I love rodeo. It's that simple."

"I don't believe you. What happened here that makes you hate it so?"

Now it was his turn to look away. He gazed toward the ranch, hoping to see the truck returning with water. "I worked like a dog here," he said. "My uncle was a harsh man. There aren't any good memories here."

"Well, *make* some," Becky demanded. "You can't ride the rodeo circuit forever."

"Make some memories," he repeated, studying her serious expression. "Just like that. You think it's that easy?"

"Why not?"

"Why not," he echoed, leaning closer to her to close the gap between them. He took her by the shoulders and kissed her long and hard. He sensed her surprise, and then her response, and her lips parted to allow him entrance. He pushed her gently onto her back and followed her down, in the shade of the tree with the smell of fresh cut hay surrounding them. The birds were quiet, but the breeze made the leaves shiver and rustle, and Becky's lips were warm and sweet. He kissed her for long moments, while he was slanted over her, his weight on his elbows. Those lovely breasts were against his chest, her arms had come round his neck, and the tree protected them from the hot afternoon sun. He kissed her again, then moved lower, to that intriguing cleft of skin between her collar, shifting his weight to allow him to touch her breast and down lower, to her waist. She kissed him back, moaning a little into his mouth as he found her lips again and tugged her shirt free of her waistband. It was easy work to release the snaps that held the shirt closed, and he slid his palm over bare skin to touch first one lace-coated breast and then the other. He cupped it gently, thumbing the sensitive nub with his thumb until Becky broke off the kiss.

"Are you telling me to stop?" he asked, wanting her more than he could remember wanting a woman before.

"This isn't what I meant by making memories," she said, her voice soft. Her lips were swollen from his kisses and her cheeks were flushed.

He dipped his head and brushed his lips against the mound of her breast above her brassiere. "You're as beautiful as I thought you'd be," he said. "It's a pretty damn good memory to me."

"I don't need any more memories," she said, lifting one hand to touch his hair and brush a lock from his forehead. "A widow has too many. I need a man who isn't going to leave. And we both know that's not you."

His smile was wry as he began to fasten the snaps he'd so easily opened. "You're too smart, Miss Becky."

"Yep." She sat up and scooted back against the tree. "I'm a real genius, all right." She looked past him toward the hill. "Here comes someone. I guess we're lucky."

Lucky? He didn't feel the least bit lucky. He felt unsettled and hot, so he reached for the last of the water and drained the bottle. Becky was right. He wasn't a man to make promises he couldn't keep, just to get a woman to go to bed with him. A woman like Becky didn't need a man like him making love to her. But, damn, he wanted to.

SHE THOUGHT about him for the rest of the afternoon. She thought about how good his fingers had felt on her skin, how his lips on her breast made her want to strip off her clothes and make love to him right there under that scraggly old tree. To hell with the hay, to hell with the future, to hell with everything. She would have made love to him and damned the consequences.

If she was a different kind of woman. Becky rolled the piecrust and wished she *was* a different kind of woman. She'd be satisfied and smiling now. She'd be soaking in the tub, reveling in the memory of having a man inside her. She would smile all through supper, a woman with a delicious secret.

There were no secrets and no bubble baths. There was piecrust, and the case of peaches that Cal had brought back from town. And there was Tommy, cranky from having a nap that was too short, and Peter, hiding on the porch so his little brother wouldn't break another one of his X-men action figures. Maude had been on the phone all afternoon, planning a camping trip that would make Will crazy and most likely entertain the cowboys. She'd learned they liked to show off a little, especially for the ladies.

She was going to have to make some decisions soon, such as where to live. And what to do when Mike asked her out again, though she wondered if he would. He'd been a little stunned by the children, a little suspicious of Will. That had been quite a date, uneventful until she'd rounded the corner of the lobby and seen Maude and Tommy. For a second she'd been afraid that something was wrong, but Maude had smiled and Becky's heart started beating again.

And then beat faster when she'd seen Will.

She had to face it, Becky decided, lifting the circle of piecrust into the pan and tucking it gently into the shape of the dish. She was attracted to the man. It was perfectly natural, after all. He was young and handsome, two assets in short supply around here. And he looked at her sometimes as if he'd like to take off her clothes and make love to her right then and there.

And now he was trying to do exactly that, but she was too smart for that. Too smart for a broken heart or hurt feelings or the kind of embarrassment that results from a man making love to you once and afterward pretending you don't exist. She would look out, she promised herself. She divided the sliced peaches between the pie plates, then covered them with circles of dough.

"Mommy! Want to get down," Tommy hollered, banging his toy.

"In a minute." She pinched the dough together, fluted the edges and carefully set the pies in the oven to bake.

"Mommy!" he cried again, obviously losing patience with his mother. Becky wiped her hands and went over to lift him from the high chair. He was a good baby, but he needed a father. Peter could con Will into playing checkers and teaching him to ride, but what did Tommy need? A strong pair of arms to lift him and a man's voice telling him it was all right when he fell down and scraped the palms of his hands on the gravel road.

Well, Becky thought, setting Tommy on the floor, there was no sense dreaming of things they weren't going to have. At least not right now. She led the boy onto the porch and sat down on the swing. Tommy went over to his favorite toy, a pile of brown wooden logs that Maude had brought from the attic. He liked to build log cabins and corrals for his collection of plastic horses. Tommy was a quiet builder, while Peter liked to be moving and doing, full of conversation and being around people. Both boys had taken to Will too easily, as if they were starved for attention.

Which wasn't true. Maude and the cowboys spoiled the children, and there was always someone to play with or talk to. That was another reason she'd hate to leave this place, Becky knew. She sat down in the swing and watched her children play. They'd found a family here, which made it even harder to walk away. But she'd learned a few years ago that nothing was guaranteed to stay the same. She was stronger now, and wiser. She had skills and references and a way to make a living.

Becky rocked herself in the swing and looked out the screened windows to the front yard. She would miss this old house, but it was time to start thinking about moving on before she made a mistake, like falling in love with the wrong man once again.

9

"HOW MANY?"

"Eight," Maude said, looking at her list. "Each one is paying one hundred and fifty dollars for the privilege, too. Including lunch and dinner on Saturday and breakfast Sunday, plus the use of the horse."

"Twelve hundred dollars?" Becky was impressed. "That's a lot of money for one camping trip."

"They voted on what they thought was a fair price, even though I told them that I would do it for free, just for the practice. No one thought that was fair, though. And they're bringing their own sleeping bags," Maude announced. "But I think we'll have to buy them from now on. We can't expect everyone to bring their own gear. How much do you think you'll need for the food?"

Becky looked down at her own list. "Eight plus the two of us. How many cowboys?"

"Decker, Malone and Will. Cal and Oatey will stay here and take care of the ranch."

"I can't go, Maude. I can't leave the kids overnight. Oatey is wonderful for short periods of time, but I don't think—"

"It's all settled. I've hired Millie Freeman's daughter-in-law. She's a mother of three, so she should be able to handle your two little ones. And she could use the money, too."

"I can't do that, Maude. It's another expense."

"It's worth it," the older woman insisted. "I need you to cook. Just driving the food up there isn't going to work, though I think that's a good plan. All right? I promise the children will be fine, and you could use a break yourself, you know."

Becky couldn't resist. After all, an overnight camping trip in the hills overlooking the summer range was something she'd never done before. "Maybe Millie's daughter-in-law, I think her name is Lisa, could come over this week and meet the children."

"Fine. I'll give you her number and you can talk to her. I think her youngest boy is the same age as Peter."

"Maybe she'd bring him with her. Peter would love company."

"There," Maude said, smiling. "Didn't I tell you it was a good idea? I'll need you to have the lunch ready, plus breakfast. You know, eggs, bacon, coffee in a metal pot over the campfire. Real ranch food."

"How about steaks for dinner? There are still plenty in the large freezer."

"Excellent." She crossed that off her list. "Now, all I have to do is talk to Will and tell him he's going to be busy next Saturday night."

"I don't know if he's going to like this," Becky cautioned. When Will wasn't haying, he spent a lot of evenings in the office, going over the accounts and questioning his mother about the way his uncle had run things around here. Apparently the books had to be in good shape for prospective buyers to examine.

"He'll be fine. Especially when I tell him that we're making money."

Becky had her doubts. "He's been working awfully hard this past week. I don't think he's taken any time off."

"Then he'll be glad of the vacation."

Becky didn't think that Will would consider escorting nine women on a camping trip much of a vacation, but she had to admire Maude's optimism. "What about dessert? Cookies are a safe bet and will travel well, though I suppose I could do an angel food cake and berries, too."

"Whatever you think, dear." Maude looked back at her list and crossed off something else. "I know this is going to be the start of something wonderful."

Becky had her doubts, but she kept them to herself.

WILL REINED UP beside Decker. "If there was a list of crazy people in Montana, I figure my name would be at the top of the list." The two men rode behind the group of gray-haired cowgirls, making sure that none of them fell off their horses. This was the same group who had herded cows a few weeks ago, but the fact that nothing had happened last time didn't reassure either man.

"Yep," Decker agreed. "You and your ma are two of a kind."

"Don't lump me in with Maude. I can't believe I let her talk me into this crazy scheme. Camping with her Dead Club," he muttered, pulling his hat low against the late-afternoon sun.

"*Not* Dead Yet," the older cowboy corrected. "That's the point. Just because we're old doesn't mean we're getting ready to take our last breath on this earth. I'm close to eighty-two now, and I'm doing okay." He patted his horse's neck. "These here foreign horses sure help my old bones, though."

"Maude's crazy about those horses." Will rode his chestnut mare, only this time without pain. His knee had healed just fine, though it twinged some when he worked eighteen-hour days. The ache in his back had been replaced by a different ache, the kind brought on by a yel-low-haired woman with big blue eyes.

"Could be a real money-maker."

"The horses?"

"Yeah, and givin' trail rides. Maude might have a good idea in this, Will. Kinda helps the cash flow along until the calves are sold."

Will glanced over toward him. "Yeah? And when did you get interested in cash flow?"

"We all chipped in to buy these horses. Kind of a re-tirement program." He grinned. "Though you chipped in the most, according to Maude."

"Yeah, without knowing it." He had to smile. All along he'd thought his mother was buying new dresses or fur-niture or anything to make her life more comfortable. Instead, she'd squirreled it away and started her own business.

"You selling the place puts a new wrinkle in our plans," Decker stated.

"I'm sorry about that." Will hated that part, and didn't know what to do about the fate of the old men, though he'd lain awake nights worrying about it. "I've got a lit-tle place outside of Billings. You're all welcome. I could add a bunkhouse."

"How big?"

He was embarrassed to tell him. "Twenty acres."

Decker chuckled. "Why, what would we do in the city?"

"Relax."

"Don't want to relax," Decker said. "We want to raise horses and look at the mountains and do a little work now and then to make sure we're still alive. Don't want to sit in your house with nothing to do except play cards."

"But where else will you go?"

"Not your concern, son," the old man replied. "You take your ma and you go back to Billings. Don't know what she'll do with herself there, though." He pointed to the crowd of women up ahead. "She's made some friends and she's bought horses and all she wants to do is stay here."

"But she's no spring chicken, Deck. She's not young enough for this kind of life anymore."

"She's doing okay. She's where she wants to be." The older man gave him a long, steady look. "Let her be."

"She'll work herself to death."

Decker shook his head. "Let her be," he repeated. "Don't be so quick to rush in here and change things." He nudged his horse and trotted off, away from Will and toward Malone. Will was left by himself, eating dust. He wasn't trying to hurt anyone, but none of them understood. There was nothing for him or Maude on this ranch now, and she'd promised to leave. Nothing ever stayed the same. This remote ranch was no place for any of them, not for old cowboys or old women or a young woman with small children. And especially not for a man who'd spent his adult life trying not to come home.

"OH, AND HE was a *huge* bear," Malone announced. "Darker than night, bigger than one of them football players you see on TV. He came up and whacked my hat off with his paw." He made a motion and his hat went flying, to land in Dr. Theresa's lap. The ladies tittered, but their attention remained on the old cowboy. Becky, standing in the background beyond the reach of the firelight, chuckled watching him. She'd heard this story before, and every time she heard it the bear got bigger and blacker, with better aim.

Malone leaned toward the light of the fire and pointed to a long scar on his temple. "Bear claw," he said. "Son of a, uh, gun caught me right there."

"What did you do next?" one woman asked, clearly awestruck.

"Well," Malone drawled, coming to his favorite part of the story. "I whacked him back. Just took my rifle and whacked him on the nose as hard as I could, and he backed up and hollered at me, then went down on all fours and took off into the brush."

"My goodness!" one woman cried. "You were so lucky."

"Yes, ma'am," Malone said, retrieving his hat and sticking it back on his bald head. "And that bear was, too, because I couldn't get my rifle in position in time and had to settle for hitting him on the nose."

Becky turned as Will came up to stand beside her. He was smiling.

"Those stories get better and better," he whispered.

"Decker is getting ready to outdo him." She nodded toward the older cowboy, who had edged closer to the fire. He leaned forward, looking impatient as the ladies started asking Malone questions about bears.

"And Deck's going to have a hard time, too." Will chuckled. "I didn't think this evening would go this well. I have to give you and Maude credit."

"Thank you." She looked over at Maude, who looked up and winked at her. Becky gave her a thumbs-up sign. "She figures if we can do this once a week we can make enough money to put a new roof on the house."

"Once a week?"

"Sure. There are plenty of people in Billings and Great Falls and even Bozeman who would like to ride around a real ranch. And *we* have special horses for those who can't be jarred. That gives us an edge."

"An edge," he repeated, shaking his head. "Do you know how many trail rides you'd have to give to pay for those fancy animals?"

She wished he wouldn't stand quite so close. "We're not including the cost of the horses, Maude said, because they were a gift."

"And, according to the records, a gift from me," he reminded her.

"Maude likes to think of it as an investment, but she doesn't like counting it into the profit and loss figures. At least," Becky added, "not until the mares foal and we can start a breeding program."

He tugged on her braid, which hung down her back between her shoulder blades, and sent little shivers down her spine. "Do you ever wear your hair loose?"

She wished he wouldn't touch her. She wished he would. "At night," she whispered.

Will lifted the braid and draped it over her shoulder. His fingers brushed the top of her breast. "Your hair must be long."

"Um, yes." She stood still when she knew she should move away. She should make sure there was enough hot water in case their guests wanted another round of whiskey-spiked hot chocolate. The tents were set up under the pine trees, the weather had cooperated with a clear sky filled with stars and the sliver of a moon. It was the kind of night meant for campfires and stories and stolen kisses in the pine-scented darkness. And she didn't need kisses, Becky told herself as she turned to Will. He wouldn't dare kiss her now, not with all these people.

Will smiled at her as if he knew what she was thinking. "If we were alone . . ." he said, letting his voice trail off.

"We wouldn't be alone. Not up here at night or any other time," she reminded him. "There is no reason for us to be alone."

"I can think of one," he said, giving the braid a little tug before releasing her. Becky didn't reply. She turned back to the campfire and pretended to be listening to Decker's story. She couldn't admit she was attracted to him, not in a physical way or any other way. They'd almost made love last week on the picnic blanket, and she'd been damn lucky she'd come to her senses in time. She didn't need a man in her life, and she didn't need this particular man.

But it was tempting, Becky thought, hiding a sigh. Sleep couldn't come soon enough. She would hide in her tent and pretend she liked being alone at night.

She would avoid him from now on.

BECKY ROSE AT DAWN to fix the coffee and get a fire going. She dressed quickly in the tent, then once outside splashed her face with cold water from a basin, brushed her teeth and rebraided her hair. She wasn't the only one up. Will came out of the brush with an armful of firewood. He hadn't shaved, but that didn't lessen his attractiveness. He wished her a good-morning and helped her build the fire. She fetched water from the nearby stream and made coffee on the propane stove as quietly as she could, then poured them each a cup.

It seemed natural to sit on the log and look at the fire while they drank their coffee and everyone else slept in tents scattered among the pine trees. Becky had shared a tent with Maude, who had confessed her exhaustion and gone immediately to sleep. Becky had lain awake worrying about the future and wondering how the boys were doing with Lisa Freeman. She'd tossed and turned within the confines of her sleeping bag before drifting into a dreamless sleep. Now it was barely dawn, and there was no telling how long the others would sleep. One of the cowboys could be heard snoring from a distant tent.

"Couldn't you sleep either?" Will asked.

"Oh, I slept fine," she lied.

"Really."

"Must be the fresh air. I wanted to get up early and get the food going. I thought if I started the bacon and got it cooked ahead, it would be easier to feed everyone."

"You're always thinking," he murmured. "Always so organized and prepared."

"I have to be. That's my job."

"Maude was lucky to have found you."

"She said she knew how I felt, what I was going through, being widowed and raising a child by herself." She stood up and started going through the large cooler for the bacon. It didn't take long to fix a couple of cast-iron skillets on the grate over the fire and start frying bacon. She didn't let Will help, which seemed to annoy him. "Did you camp much when you were a boy?"

"Some," he said, pouring himself a fresh cup of coffee. "In the summers, when the herd was up here I'd come up and ride fence and check the cattle. Then I'd stay, if it got late. I liked it. It was always peaceful, just like it is now." He stood and looked down at the valley below them. In the distance a tiny ribbon of road was all that could be seen in the pale light of early morning.

Becky set up the food on the folding metal table she'd brought from the ranch. She'd covered it with a red gingham cloth to give it a Western look and last night's buffet and steaks fresh from the campfire had met with no complaints. Today she would serve blueberry muffins, with bowls of fresh strawberries and chunks of melon. The ladies would have their eggs cooked to order, their bacon hot and crispy. There were leftover cookies for those who wanted to take a snack for the ride back to the ranch, and jugs of lemonade the cowboys would pack for a rest stop on the way down the mountain later.

They kept bumping into each other, something that was both pleasant and embarrassing. "How do you want your eggs?"

"Fried." He reached for the carton of eggs. "I can do it myself."

"Are you trying to make me look bad?" she teased, reaching for the carton and taking it away from him. "I'm the camp cook here."

"We were always taught that the cook was the boss." Will smiled, giving her a look that made her knees wobble alarmingly. "So I guess I'll have to do what you say."

"It's about time you realized that." She put the bacon into one pan and cracked the eggs into the empty one.

He followed her over to the campfire and sat down to watch her cook. "I'm a slow learner."

She turned to face him. "We can do this, you know. We can make this ranch work with trail rides and camp outs, plus the income from the calves and from selling a Paso or two."

"I'm not arguing that someone could do that," Will insisted. "All I'm saying is that my mother isn't young enough to do it and you can't do it alone or with a handful of old cowboys who can't see past their horses' ears."

"But—"

"'Morning!" Maude called, coming up behind them. "I swear the smell of coffee woke me up." She peered past Becky's shoulder. "Looks like my son has the first breakfast."

Becky flipped the eggs over before turning to Maude. "How did you sleep?"

"Just fine. I'm a little stiff," she admitted, stretching her arms above her head, "but the fresh air does wonders for a good night's sleep." She clapped her hand on Will's shoulder as he began to stand. "Stay where you are. I'm going to get some coffee."

"Take the log," he said. "I'll get your coffee."

She winked at Becky and did as she was told. "How long have you two been up?"

"Not long."

"Long enough to have a difference of opinion, I see."

"Just a discussion," Becky said, reaching for Will's tin plate.

"Is he flirting with you?"

Becky blushed. "No, of course not. Maude, for heaven's sake!"

Will returned with the coffee and handed it to his mother. "Why is Becky blushing?" Becky gave him his breakfast and he sat down on another log and looked at both women.

"She's too close to the fire, that's all," his mother explained. "It's chilly up here this morning."

"It won't be in a couple of hours," he said, digging into his eggs.

The talk turned to the weather, and Becky gratefully slipped away from the fire. Spending too much time with Will was dangerous, and she'd be better off remembering that fact from now on.

HE WATCHED HER work, watched the kind way she treated
their guests and the way people responded. The cowboys loved her, and she took care of them in a way that
didn't make them feel old. Maude depended on her, that
was obvious. They all did. He wondered what she would
do when she left the SV, where she would go and if her
employers would appreciate her the way they should.

He wanted her, with a fierce protective lust he'd never
experienced before. He watched her move around the
campfire and pour coffee and serve food to the gray-
haired ladies and he wanted nothing more than to take
her into the nearest tent and make love to her.

After he unbraided that yellow hair, of course.

She was aware of him, too. They were the two youngest people on that side of the mountain, both single and
healthy. Some of the women had looked at both of them
with knowing looks and smiles, something he could do
without. He wasn't going to grab Becky by the hair and
drag her off into the woods in front of everyone, but
damn it, he was going to kiss her before the morning was
out because she was driving him crazy.

Ever since that afternoon in the hay meadow, he'd
thought about making love to her. He'd thought about
taking it slow or doing it fast and hard. He'd thought
about that hair falling across his chest and he'd thought
about how he'd feel inside her. And he'd resolved to stay
away from her, because she wasn't the kind of woman a
man like him should make love to.

He hadn't slept much.

"Will," Maude said, sounding impatient.

"What?"

"Don't snap at me. I've been trying to get your attention for three minutes now, and you're glaring at the
campfire."

He looked down at her and forced himself to concentrate. "Sorry. I was thinking."

"Well, forget that for a while. I need to ask you a favor."

"Sure. What?"

"Becky's going to need help packing all this stuff back to the truck. Can you stay and help her? You can catch up with us afterward."

"Can't Malone or Decker do it?" He frowned. He didn't want to be alone with her, not really. Fantasizing was fine, but he wasn't made of steel either.

"No. I need Decker with the horses and J.J.'s arthritis is bothering him this morning."

"Which leaves me," he stated flatly. "If you're thinking you're going to get me to fall for Becky and stay here on the ranch, you're wrong."

"Will!" Maude's eyes widened. "You're all wrong for Becky. You're not at all her type." She patted him on the arm before she returned to her friends. "Just carry the boxes, dear. And catch up with us when you can."

Not Becky's type? What the hell was that supposed to mean? He frowned once again and headed toward the horses. If the men were so damn sick, he guessed they'd need help saddling up the animals.

Decker grinned when he saw him. "Mighty fine mornin'."

"Yeah?"

"Well, I thought so," the old man said. "You get cleanup duty?"

"Yeah."

"Thought so. Miss Becky's going to need some help packing this stuff out."

"So I heard."

"You mind your manners, now," Decker said. "You'll scare the ladies with that look on your face, like you wish you could shoot somethin'."

Will ignored him and reached for a bridle. There were a lot of things he'd like to do, but none of them involved shooting. And all of them involved Becky McGregor.

THREE HOURS AFTER the women had awakened, they rode off down the mountain toward home. Well-fed and feeling like they had had an adventure, they were on their way back to the ranch house, where they would climb off their horses and, according to Maude, rush to the telephone to tell their friends, who would also want to book trips up the mountain, of course. Theresa took photographs to send to a nephew who worked for a travel magazine.

"From rags to riches," Maude said, kissing her son goodbye before she got on her horse. "We're on our way now."

It was no time to argue, Will decided, not when Maude was smiling at him and looking so pleased with herself. "I'm glad you had a good time."

"You did, too, my boy," Maude said. "I could tell."

"Yes." He couldn't argue that fact. "I always liked camping up here, and it was good to hear the stories again and sleep under the stars."

She leaned over and kissed him on the cheek. "This is your home," she said, straightening once again.

"Yes, ma'am," Will said, stepping away so she could follow the others. He stood on the ridge and watched them ride for a few minutes. Decker was in the lead this time, the others following at their own pace. Maude rode beside one of the taller women, the doctor maybe, and Malone brought up the rear. They were in no hurry and were even going to stop for a snack along the way. Will returned to the campsite and started toward Becky. He promised himself he would be all business, would pack her up, carry the stuff the mile or so to the car, then leave.

He would not touch her, even though they were alone on a mountain with only the summer wind for company. He would stay far away and carry what she told him to carry. He was hers to command.

"You don't have to do anything," she said. "I can manage. Really."

Will looked at the table and boxes and the two coolers, then back at one of the most maddening women in Montana. "You're going to get all this stuff to the car by yourself? You're parked a mile away, easy."

"I have plenty of time." She folded the tablecloth and set it in one of the boxes.

"Why, Miss Becky, if I didn't know better I'd think you were trying to get rid of me."

She looked up then and saw his smile. "And you'd be right. Really, I can do this myself. Go on with the others."

"But what about the bears?" He stepped closer and gazed down into those blue eyes. "And mountain lions, too. Didn't you listen to Deck's story?"

Becky smiled, and Will felt his heart flip over inside his chest. "I listened, all right. I happen to be used to hearing cowboys tell tall tales."

He touched her cheek, ran his finger along her jaw and wondered at the softness of her skin. "If I told you I didn't sleep last night for wanting you, would you think it was another tall tale?"

"I'd be sure of it," she whispered, but she didn't move away from his touch. He lifted her chin with his index finger and bent down to kiss her. Before he touched his lips to hers, he paused.

"It's true," he said, brushing his lips against hers in a teasing motion. He waited for a reaction from her. Would she pull away or kiss him back?

"I have work to do," she said, but her hands touched his arms and crept upward.

"Like what?" His lips moved to her cheek, to her ear, to the long column of her neck. She smelled like coffee and sunshine and her skin was soft against his tongue.

"Oh, lots of things," she said, closing her eyes as his lips returned to hers.

He kissed her for a long moment, until her arms went around his neck and her body was against his.

"Over here," he said, breaking the embrace and taking her hand. He led her to his bedroll, still open underneath the pine tree.

"We're crazy," she said, looking at the bed and then at him. "I don't do things like this."

"I won't make love to you if you don't want me to." He meant it. He'd never forced a woman, never seduced someone to do what she didn't want to do. His fingers touched her shirt, unsnapped the first snap, then the second.

"I want you to," she admitted. "That's what's so crazy. I keep telling myself that it's wrong."

He opened two more snaps, pulled the shirttails from her waistband, slid his hands around her bare waist. "Why?"

"I've never made love on a mountain before."

Will smiled down at her. "Haven't you ever done anything completely wild, something that made no sense but just felt right?"

"Is that how you describe what we're doing right now?"

He slipped the shirt off her shoulders to reveal a white lace bra and tantalizing breasts. "Yes. Tell me this isn't what you want. What we both want."

Becky felt the warmth of the sun on her skin and suddenly felt free. And young and sexy and desirable. She was alone on a mountain with a man who clearly desired her. A man she desired, too. She reached for him then, unbuttoning his shirt the way he had undone hers, slipping the sleeves from his arms and sliding them off his hands. She smoothed her palms over his furred chest, tracing the scars she found there.

He moaned when she touched his skin, when she kissed the jagged scar above his belt buckle. Within minutes they had managed to take each other's clothes off, though Becky didn't know how they did it, not with belt buckles and jeans and boots to contend with. But he was naked above her, her skin was on fire, and she pulled him closer because she couldn't touch him enough. She felt him hot and hard against her thigh, ready to make love to her, when he pulled away and looked down into her eyes.

"I didn't bring anything," he gasped. "This is going to be a problem."

"Yes," Becky said, staring into those dark eyes. She tried to hide her disappointment and how much of an idiot she felt. Now was not the time to tell him that she was a woman who got pregnant as easily as a brood mare.

"Damn," he said, touching his lips to one breast, then the other. "I should have thought about this."

This exquisite torture, she decided, was not for the fainthearted. "The first aid kit," Becky said. "There's one with the kitchen gear."

"You think there's a condom in the kitchen?" He smiled down at her.

"It's worth a try."

"Don't move," he ordered, lifting himself off her. "And cross your fingers."

She closed her eyes instead, wondering if fate was playing some kind of cruel joke. Wondering if she should be crossing her legs instead, or pulling on her clothes and running like hell down the other side of the ridge to the truck. She was a sensible woman, a mother, a widow, and she lay naked on a bedroll in the middle of nowhere hoping her handsome cowboy-about-to-be-lover could find a condom.

She should be ashamed of herself.

"Hey," Will whispered, lying next to her. "You can open your eyes now."

"No. I don't think I'd better. I think I've come to my senses," she muttered. "I think I should get dressed, but I'm too embarrassed to move." She felt his lips brush her bare shoulder and she shivered.

"You're beautiful."

She couldn't speak, because he'd lowered his mouth to her breasts, first one and then the other, sending sparks of need through her body. He took her hands away from her abdomen and kissed the skin there, and then lower. When she would have protested, he captured her wrists in one hand and held her still while he sought what she would have kept from him. He urged her thighs apart with a gentle hand, then touched her with his lips and tongue until she could no longer protest. Until she was weak with longing and desire, slick with readiness for him. His fingers touched her, sending a lance of intense pleasure through her, making her moan.

He rose above her then. "You were right," he said. "There were some condoms in there, though God knows why." And Becky opened her eyes.

"Thank goodness," she answered, looking into his dark eyes, seeing the passion that echoed her own. He took her then, sliding slowly into her with a breathtaking ease that made her gasp.

He hesitated, frowning. "Am I hurting you?"

"No." She reached for his hips to draw him closer. "It's just . . . been a long time. I was surprised, that's all."

Will touched her lips with his. "You feel so good. Just the way I imagined." He moved within her again, deeper this time, until he filled her completely. He moved again, slowly, waiting for her response.

Her fingers tightened on his skin as he made long, slow love to her. She lifted her hips to meet him, answered his need with her own, until the world came to a dizzying peak and tossed them both over the edge into someplace familiar and strange and dazzling, all at once.

10

IT WAS WITHOUT a doubt the best morning she'd had in a very long time, Becky mused. Though it most likely wasn't morning any longer, from the sun shining high in the sky. She lay snuggled beside Will on the bedroll, the gingham tablecloth tossed over their naked bodies. She wondered when the others would make it back to the ranch, and if anyone would miss the cook or the boss. It was a two-hour ride, but they were stopping for snacks and getting their pictures taken at Silver Creek. Surely it hadn't been an hour since they'd ridden off, though Becky thought her world had certainly shifted in a short period of time.

She turned toward Will, who opened his eyes and smiled at her. "Come here," he said, shifting so her head rested on his shoulder.

"I wonder what time it is," she said, relishing the feel of her skin against his.

"Does it matter?"

"I guess not." Did she dare be irresponsible and decadent just a little while longer? "I don't have to fix lunch."

He chuckled. "Are you always thinking about food?" His fingers began to stroke her breasts. Becky closed her eyes and felt a swift longing to have him inside of her again.

"No," she managed to say, as his hand trailed lower, across her abdomen. "I can't believe we did . . . what we just did."

"What we're still doing," he corrected, touching her where she was still moist from their lovemaking. "What we're going to do again."

"But—"

He cut off her protests with a quick kiss. "As soon as we go down that mountain you'll go back to being a mother and a cook and a foreman—"

"You're the foreman now," she reminded him.

"And I'll go back to being a son and a boss and—"

"A pain in the rear," she finished for him. "You're *especially* good at that."

His brown eyes twinkled as he looked down at her, his face only inches from hers. "That's not what I was going to say." She shrugged her bare shoulders and he placed a kiss on one of them. "We're not finished here, lady."

"So the first aid kit was well-stocked?"

Will nodded. "Yes. I'd like to know which one of the men thought he would need them."

"You'll have to replace them so no one knows," she said, realizing that they could be caught after all. She didn't want the men to know that she and Will had made love. The men's clumsy attempts at matchmaking hadn't been aimed at sexual activity. She knew they hoped that something wonderful would happen, like Will staying forever. The cowboys were romantics; Becky wasn't.

"I'll bet my championship belt buckle that no one around here is going to miss them." He nudged her hips closer until their bodies were touching from chest to toe. Becky sighed with pure contentment, and Will Cody made love to her once again.

SHE MANAGED TO sneak upstairs and shower while
Maude and her friends held an impromptu meeting of the
club. Of course, she'd greeted Peter and thanked Lisa
Freeman and checked to see that Tommy was still taking
a nap before she'd hurried to her room to clean up. Peter
had been invited to go home with the Freemans for the
rest of the day, which Becky gave him permission to do.
It seemed that Josh and Peter had become instant friends
who couldn't bear to be separated. She had kissed him
goodbye and promised Lisa she'd pick him up before six.
It was Sunday, after all, and a trip to town could fit into
the schedule with little trouble.

She hadn't been missed, she realized with no small
feeling of relief. No one had said, "What were you doing
on that mountain all that time?"

No one had mentioned that she and Will had been together. Alone. For several hours. No one noticed that her
cheeks were flushed and her eyes sparkled with a secret.
She looked at herself in the mirror and felt positively ridiculous.

She wasn't in love with him, of course. Now *that*
would be foolish, falling for a footloose rodeo rider. She
certainly didn't need another man who couldn't stay in
one place for more than a couple of months. Will Cody
would be driving off in his truck, his horse trailer behind him, heading back to his own world very soon.

Becky unbraided her hair, stepped in the shower and
rinsed off the itchy bits of leaves and dirt stuck to her
skin. What they had done was a crazy fluke, something
that would never happen again. In fact, Becky resolved,
she would have to have more willpower from now on.

"WELL?" MAUDE LEANED closer to Theresa, who perched
on the sofa beside her. "What do you think?"

"They had sex, all right," the doctor pronounced. "Written all over her face."

Maude nodded. Becky thought she'd sneaked upstairs with no one the wiser, but she'd had to talk to that nice Freeman woman, of course. She'd had to let Maude know she was back. And she'd looked a little flushed and rumpled, too, which was another good sign. "That's what I thought, too. She was in a big hurry to get out of here and get in the shower."

"There were leaves in her hair."

Which was a very good sign. At least her son and Becky had been up to something there in those woods. "I'd give a lot to see what my son looks like."

"I'll bet," Theresa drawled, "that he's a tired young man who is most likely quite pleased with himself. But men are better at hiding these things."

Maude looked doubtful. She'd always thought it was the other way around. "You think so?"

"We could take a walk out back and go see for ourselves."

"Maybe when the others leave," Maude said. Several of her guests were still drinking lemonade and discussing how they would organize looking at each other's photographs. There was also the matter of the old-fashioned barn dance to consider. Things were definitely looking up.

HE WASN'T IN LOVE with her, of course. He respected the way she worked so hard, and he damned well enjoyed her cooking. She was a good-looking woman with a way with animals and people, and the sex, well, he'd never experienced anything quite like that before. Of course, he hadn't been with a woman in many long months. And there was something about making love outdoors that could have had that effect. Next time he would untie that braid, he promised himself.

"'Bout time you got back," Decker said, standing in the door. "We've been entertaining the ladies with one man short."

"I'm not much for entertaining," Will said, dismounting. He unpacked his gear, unsaddled the mare and, as Decker opened the corral gate, set her free to run in the pasture. He turned toward his friend. "I thought the ladies had left."

"Nope. They're still in the house, chatterin' away about their big adventure."

"Maude's happy, then?"

"Yep. She's just about over the moon."

Will put his hands on his hips and surveyed the ranch buildings. Half were coated with fresh white paint, the others were a dusty gray. "I guess if you didn't know any better, you'd be impressed."

Decker didn't smile. "There's someone here waiting for you."

"Becky got back? Good."

The old cowboy shook his head. "Not Becky. She came home a while ago and is in the house with the women. There's a man here to see you, says a real estate agency in Billings sent him out here. Said you had an appointment."

Will winced. He'd forgotten about that. "Hell," he swore. "That was set up weeks ago. Must have slipped my mind."

"Yeah, well, he's been walking around, looking things over. I kept him out of Maude's sight. Didn't want to upset her."

"Thanks."

Decker continued to frown at him. "Didn't do it for you," he said. "Did it for Maude. Don't want her day ruined."

"Yeah." Will should have felt relief that a prospective buyer had finally shown up. He couldn't remember the man's name, but he wished him to hell right now. "I'll take care of it."

"Last time I saw him he was over by the bunkhouse. Drove up in one of them shiny new Jeeps, wears shiny new boots."

Will sighed. Of course, anything shiny was suspicious to an eighty-year-old cowhand. "I'll go find him."

He wondered why he felt a little sick to his stomach. He'd eaten too many eggs, that's all. He'd had the kind of morning most men could only dream of and now it was time to come back to earth and face what he had to do. Trouble was, he'd had too much time to think on the ride home. And he didn't like the ideas that had occurred to him, either. It was best, Will decided, striding toward the bunkhouse, to keep his mind on his original plan and not get sidetracked by women, but he'd told himself that before and it hadn't helped a bit. He was damned if he did and damned if he didn't and damned if he stayed on this ranch a minute longer.

And he was damned if he knew what to do with the real estate agent.

BECKY PUT ON a dress. She told herself it was Sunday and she was tired of blue jeans and clothes that smelled like horse. She would do laundry, she would sit on the porch and play with Tommy. She braided her damp hair and wondered if it would ever rain. Maybe she would take Tommy with her when she went to town; they would have ice cream and she would try to forget that she had made love to Will Cody this morning. Twice. And it had been incredibly satisfying and, all in all, surprising in many ways.

She lifted Tommy from his crib, changed his diaper, and took him downstairs. There was a breeze on the porch, and the house was dark and silent. Maude must have drawn the shades against the afternoon sun after her guests had gone home. Becky sat in the swing while Tommy found the box of miniature logs and plastic horses that were kept in the corner. Lady, stretched out in front of the door, lifted her head to see who was coming. When Peter didn't appear, she put her head down between her paws, sighed and closed her eyes.

"Daddy's horse," Tommy said, lifting a horse to show his mother.

Becky shook her head. "Mr. Cody's horse, Tommy. Not daddy."

The toddler ignored her. "Daddy's horse," he repeated, making the horse move across the wooden floor. He stood up and, stepping over the dog, went to the screen door, the horse clutched in his chubby fist. "Daddy!" he called. "Come here!"

There was no arguing with the child, Becky decided. He was convinced that Will was his father and, with a toddler's stubborn defiance, continued to call the man "Daddy" every time he saw him. Becky looked outside and watched as Will walked a short, stocky man to his car. She didn't recognize the man who shook Will's hand so seriously and handed him what looked like a business card before getting in his Jeep, but that didn't mean anything. He could be the contractor giving a bid on the new roof, or that lawyer who had been trying to contact Will with no luck. Maybe he'd given up trying to get him on the phone and had decided to come out to the ranch.

Tommy let out a bone-chilling scream of great joy. "Daddy!"

Lady whimpered and tried to move away from the child without knocking him over. Becky watched as Will looked toward the porch, then started in their direction. Tommy would have screamed himself blue if Will had turned in the opposite direction.

Maude stepped out on the porch, and Becky turned to greet her. The older woman sat down in the big leather chair and looked very upset. "Something wrong?"

"Yes," Maude said, sighing.

"I thought your camp out was a big success."

"It was, but I've just about had it with that boy," she said, as Will drew closer to the porch and started up the steps.

"With Will?" Did Maude know about this morning? Becky took a deep breath and tried to look casual as the cowboy carefully opened the door without knocking over his littlest fan. Lady took advantage of the chance to flee to a deserted corner. Will picked up Tommy and admired the plastic horse before turning to the women.

"I guess the ladies all left?" he asked. Tommy took off his hat and placed it on his own head.

Becky nodded, suddenly unable to put two words together. He wore the same shirt she'd taken off him this morning and the sight of those buttons did something to her heartbeat.

"I guess *your* company left, too?" Maude echoed, glaring at him. Will winced and set Tommy on the floor.

"Go find some more horses, kid," he said gently. Tommy kept the hat and grinned, content to have his hero in the same room. Then Will sat beside Becky in the swing, keeping a careful, polite distance between them. "Yes."

"Who was that man?"

"A real estate agent from Billings. He'd been sent here to look over the property. There are several people interested in it already."

"How convenient for you," Maude said, looking as if she'd like nothing better than to take him over her knee and spank the living daylights out of him. "And what about us? Where do we all fit into this?"

Will leaned forward, making the swing rock in a gentle motion. He planted his boots on the floor and stopped the movement. "I give up," he said, running one hand through his hair. "I'm done, finished, through."

Maude raised her eyebrows. "What exactly does that mean?"

Which is what Becky would have asked, if her tongue could move and form words.

"You can keep this place, if you want to live here so badly. I'll spend the next few weeks fixing it up the best I can before I leave. I'll get my deposit back on your condo and use it for the new roof. You and the others can stay here as long as you want to." He shrugged. "I can't fight you anymore on this, though I still think running this place is too big a job." He glanced toward Becky and added, "For all of you."

She should have felt relief. She and the boys still had a home; she still had a job. Nothing would change. But the words *before I leave* beat a painful rhythm in her heart. *Before I leave.* In a few weeks. "A new roof," was what she said, her voice sounding hollow even to her own ears. "That would be wonderful."

Every wrinkle in Maude's face headed upward as she smiled at her son. "Nothing's going to change?" she asked, as if having to hear the words again.

"No. I'll keep sending you money. You can do what you need to with it," he said, rubbing his palms on his thighs as if he was nervous. "But I'd hold off on the expensive horses for a while. And the minute your doctor tells me you shouldn't be living out here, then it's off to Billings with me, understand?"

Becky wanted to reach over and put her hand over his and tell him he had done the right thing, but she clasped her hands together in her lap.

"I understand perfectly," Maude said. She rose and kissed her son, who stood up and hugged his mother and patiently listened to her tell him she was relieved and happy and could now go forward and have an old-fashioned barn dance to celebrate.

"This calls for a drink," Maude announced, smiling at the two of them. "I'll be right back," she called, hurrying into the house.

Will sat down again in the swing, this time a few inches closer. She wondered if he did that on purpose. He reached over and took her hand and looked down at her fingers.

Becky waited for him to say something, but he remained silent. "Why did you change your mind?" she asked finally.

"I'm not sure."

Which was not the answer she'd hoped to hear.

"I guess it's because I've never seen her so happy," Will said. "I had a lot of time to think on the way down the mountain today." He smiled his very handsome smile. "I was in the mood to think about things." He released her hand, placing it back on her thigh. "Are you okay?"

"Sure." He was leaving, he was smiling, he was acting as if this morning was nothing more than a pleasant sex-

ual encounter between consenting adults. Which, of
course, it was. And nothing more.

"I wondered—"

"Here we go," Maude said, carrying a tray of glasses,
a pitcher of iced tea and a bottle of whiskey through the
door. She set it down on the battered table beside the
chair. "What would you like?"

"Tea is fine," Becky said, wishing she could have
something stronger, but she had to go to town in a while.
It would be good to get away from here, she decided,
taking the glass Maude handed to her. She could use the
time with her children. She could start acting like someone with a brain again.

"Will?"

"Just a swallow for me," he said. "I'm taking Becky out
to dinner tonight."

She turned back toward him. "You are?"

"If Maude will baby-sit, that is. You're wearing a dress.
Shame to waste it."

The older woman handed her son a glass. "Of course
I will. How lovely for the two of you to go out."

"I can't," Becky said. "I have to pick up Peter in a few
hours and—"

"I have to shave and shower, so we're not in any hurry.
We'll go out after we get Pete," Will stated. "Unless you're
too tired."

She met his gaze and saw the teasing light in his dark
eyes. He was daring her to refuse him, knowing she
wouldn't admit she was tired—from either last night's
camping trip or this morning's lovemaking. "I'm not that
tired," she said, wondering what he was up to. Surely this
couldn't be a real date. Maybe he thought that after this
morning he owed her a meal.

A reverse date.

"Don't look so suspicious." He laughed. "My mother will think I'm up to no good."

Maude lifted her glass. "To the success of the ranch."

Will sighed, but touched his glass to Maude's, then Becky's. "To your continued good health," he added.

"And to a new roof," Becky said.

"Daddy," Tommy said, hurrying over to Will and standing in between the man's knees. "Can I have drink too?"

"Here," Becky said, holding her glass to his lips.

Will sighed and took his hat from the child's head. "Can't you get him to stop calling me that?"

"I've tried and tried, but he won't stop."

He lifted the child onto his lap. "Tommy, I'm not your daddy."

Tommy grinned and took the hat back. "Daddy's hat," he said, grinning at the women.

Maude chuckled. "Maybe you'd better give up on that little problem, too. As long as you're in the mood to mellow."

"Mellow?" He gently pried the brim of his hat from Tommy's grip and set it on his head. "I'm not mellowing. I'm just backing up a little."

"Whatever," his mother said, taking a healthy sip of her drink. "It's a distinct improvement."

Sex will do that, Becky mused. It must take the edges off a man who figures he has too much on his mind. Or else it made him in a hurry to leave.

"I DIDN'T EXPECT this," Becky said, setting her menu aside. "Do you always feed the women you make love to?"

Will met her gaze. Those blue eyes held an expression that looked vulnerable, despite her calm manner. They sat at a corner table of the Coach House, the only decent restaurant in town, and half-empty because it was a Sunday night. "That's one of those trick questions," he drawled. "If I say yes it means I make love to a lot of women. If I say no it means I'm a cheap bastard who lets his women starve." He smiled to show he was teasing, but Becky didn't smile back.

"I apologize," she said instead, taking a sip of water from the tall stemmed glass. "I'm feeling awkward."

He wasn't. In fact, he was feeling that he definitely wanted to make love to her again, but he was smart enough to keep that thought to himself. "Don't," he said. "I thought you'd enjoy eating someone else's cooking." *I thought it was time I had you all to myself again.* Her hair was tied with one of those colored cloth things in a low ponytail, and her dress was a shade darker than her eyes. With the rose lipstick and those gold earrings, she almost looked like a stranger.

"I would, but I didn't want you to feel that you owed me anything because of what happened this—"

"Becky," he said, stopping her from finishing. "You're a beautiful woman and I'm glad you let me take you out. Can we leave it at that?"

Her cheeks flushed a becoming shade of pink as the waitress hurried over to take their order.

"Will Cody?" She peered at him from behind thick glasses. Her hair was red and curly, her face round and familiar.

"Uh, Lynn?"

She grinned. "Lynn Kelly, that's right." She looked over at Becky. "We went to high school together. A long time ago!"

"Yeah," Will answered, wishing he'd picked a different restaurant. He'd managed to avoid seeing anyone he knew these past weeks and he'd hoped to keep it that way. "How've you been?"

"Fine, fine. Married. With three children, two girls and a boy."

"Congratulations."

"Thank you. You know him. Jeff Carson? His twin sister was Lily Carson. Didn't we double date to one of the proms?"

Oh, hell. Of all the restaurants, he had to get Lily Carson's sister-in-law for a waitress. "Yeah, I think so."

She lowered her voice. "That was a shame about you and Lily. She left town right after graduation and went to live with her aunt and uncle in Seattle. Has just the one child. Never married." Lynn looked over at Becky. "Hi there. Don't you work out at Silver Valley?"

"Yes. I'm Becky McGregor."

"I *thought* you looked familiar. Glad you came in for dinner tonight."

"Thank you."

Will had had enough socializing. "Tell Jeff I said hello."

She grinned again. "I'll do that, Will." She picked up her pad, took their orders and hurried back to the kitchen. "Help yourself to the salad bar," she called over her shoulder, and Will stood up.

"I'm starving," he lied in a hearty voice. "Want your salad now?"

Becky gave him an odd look. "All right."

He didn't know what he piled on his plate, but it looked edible. Becky took her time, seeming to enjoy the array of food laid out for her to choose. He waited patiently, glad to see that she was having a good time. When they had taken their seats again, he attempted to steer the conversation toward the new horses. Becky didn't go along with him.

"So, you have a past," she teased. "I'm finding it hard to picture you as a teenager."

"Then don't." He knew he sounded rude, and cleared his throat. "Tell me about the horses. Where did you hear about Pasos?"

Becky ignored his question. "Who was Lily? Your first girlfriend?"

"Yes." He speared a forkful of salad and began to eat.

Her eyebrows rose. "A touchy subject, I see."

He shrugged. "Why should it be?"

"I don't know. You tell me."

Will considered her request, then figured he'd have no peace until he answered a question or two. Women were too curious by half. "Lily—" he paused, not pleased with having to speak her name "—was my high school girl-friend. We broke up before I left town."

"Did she break your heart or did you break hers?"

"Let's say it was a mutual decision." There. That should just about do it. He looked down at his plate and eyed the spoonful of cottage cheese he'd somehow cho-sen. There was no way in hell he was going to eat it, so he pushed his plate away and reached for his water.

"Did you leave town because of her?"

"Not exactly. My uncle was the problem there." Will frowned, remembering, and wished he hadn't. "I never thought of leaving," he admitted. "At least, I thought of going for a while and then coming back. I was cocky and full of adventure and I wanted to get out and see the world. I never thought that leaving meant never being able to return." He'd never thought his uncle would have been so willing to believe the worst.

Becky gave him a sympathetic look. "Your uncle must have been a very difficult man."

"Yeah. He was always looking for the bad, no matter what."

"Here's some nice hot rolls," Lynn chirped, dropping the basket in the middle of the table. "Anything else I can get for you?"

"I think we're all set," Will said, trying to smile. He hoped like hell she wouldn't start talking about high school again. That's what had gotten him into this mess in the first place. "Thanks."

"Oh, you're welcome." She patted him on the shoulder. "It's just so *good* to see you again. I can't wait to tell Jeff." With that, she moved on to another table of diners.

"She seems nice," Becky commented.

"Yeah." He didn't want to talk about Lynn and he didn't want to talk about Lily and he sure as hell didn't want to talk about himself. He'd brought Becky here to find out more about her, to be able to talk to her without distractions. Without Maude and the children, Decker and the rest of the men. He didn't know what he wanted to say to her, but he wanted to be able to look at her in peace. "You said you weren't married long."

She looked surprised at the shift in conversation. "No, not really."

"Is that hard for you?"

"Is what hard for me?"

"Not having a husband."

Becky put down her fork and considered the question. "We had our . . . difficulties," she admitted. "The marriage was in trouble and we were trying to work our way through it. The sad thing is that we never got a chance to find out if we could have made it work." She studied him from across the table. "Now it's my turn to ask a question." He nodded. "What made you decide to keep the ranch?"

"Guess I was tired of being the villain."

"No," she said. "There's more to it than that. You're happy here."

He laughed. "No, ma'am, I don't think that's the reason."

"Why not?"

"It's just not, that's all." Lame, even to his ears. "Maude's the one who's happy, for now. I expect she'll tire of this dude ranch business within a year or two."

"Maybe. Or maybe you'll get tired of rodeo." He watched her tuck a strand of golden hair behind her ear and wished he could touch her.

"I'm not a family man, Becky," he whispered.

Her smile was sad. "I know. When are you leaving?"

"After I arrange for the new roof and fix a few other things that could give you trouble this winter. Then I'll be on my way." He paused, then plunged in with what he wanted to tell her. "You told me last week that I should make some good memories, to replace the bad ones. You were right, and this morning was something I'll always remember."

She took a deep breath, and smiled. "Me, too."

His heart tumbled over and settled in his throat. He wished he was anywhere else but in a restaurant so he could lean over and kiss her. He couldn't be in love with her—he never fell in love, avoided it by sheer will-power—but lust was a powerful substitute. And lust was all it could be.

11

BECKY DIDN'T WANT to be in love with Will Cody. In fact, she just plain refused to be. She ignored the way Peter followed him around, begging for either a riding lesson or a checkers game. She pretended she didn't see Tommy Lee's excitement each morning when he spotted his "daddy" drinking coffee at the kitchen table. She tried very hard to forget about that morning under the pine tree and, lying alone in her bed at night, she'd had time to regret those hours.

Better not to have known passion again, if she could only have it for such a short time, she decided, after two weeks of pretending Will was nothing more to her than the owner of the SV and the man who had seen that the old ranch house sported a new roof. He'd done other things too, such as insulating water pipes to prevent the water freezing this winter, and buying Maude a new mattress. He'd replaced the old gas stove with a new model, much to Becky's surprise, and cleaned up the back porch. Decker was going to paint it white come fall.

Oh, they all agreed the summer was a good one after all. The horses were healthy and the calves were growing and the hay lay in neat round rolls, ready for winter. The bunkhouse was painted, the wooden floor covered with a new braided rug ordered from the Sears catalog. The men's bathroom had had new plumbing installed. It seemed there was nothing Will Cody couldn't do.

Except stay in one place.

Becky wiped the perspiration from her forehead with her shirtsleeve and continued to can tomatoes. She'd bought several flats of tomatoes in town the other day, and it wasn't hard to process them. Just messy, with blanching them to remove the skins, and making sure the canning jars were ready. She liked lining them up on the counter after they were finished and waiting for the satisfying *pop* that announced the lid had sealed properly.

"How pretty," Maude said, entering the kitchen and surveying the tomato-filled jars lined up on the counter. "My goodness, you did all this while I slept. I should feel very guilty."

"I'm not done yet," Becky told her. "I think I can get another dozen quarts done this afternoon."

"It's awfully hot in here."

"And hotter outside," Becky assured her. "I think everyone is taking it easy this afternoon. Which is good."

"Where are the children?"

"Peter took a ride to the creek with Will, and Tommy is still upstairs asleep. I put the fan in his room, which seemed to help."

Maude went over to the refrigerator and took out a pitcher of iced tea and a tray of ice cubes. "Come sit for a minute, Becky. Can you take a break?"

Becky turned her back on the sink full of tomatoes. "Sure," she said, grabbing two glasses from the cupboard. "Why not?" She sat down across from Maude and watched the older woman pour tea into the glasses.

"Is anything wrong?"

"No," Becky replied, taking a sip of the drink. "Why?"

"You've been quiet lately. And truthfully, dear, you look a bit pale."

"I'm fine. Just a headache."

Maude nodded. "I see. So my son hasn't done anything to . . . upset you?"

"Of course not. How could he?"

"Well." The older woman hesitated. "I suppose he could have done *something*. I thought it was so nice that you two went out to dinner."

"Maude." Becky sighed. "Please tell me you're not matchmaking. If you are, you have to know it wouldn't work."

"Why not?"

"We're too different."

"Didn't you have a good time?"

"Sure." To get her off the subject, Becky said, "We met an old high school friend of his. Lynn Kelly. She was our waitress, said she went to school with Will, that they had double-dated to a prom. Will didn't look too happy talking about it."

Maude shook her head. "I never knew what happened, but I always figured it had to do with some girl."

"Someone named Lily?"

"How did you know that?"

"That's the person Lynn mentioned." Becky had to ask. "Was she the reason Will left town?"

"I don't know," Maude answered, looking sad. "He never said, and my brother refused to talk about it. I wondered, though, if, well, never mind."

"What?"

Maude shook her head. "For a while I thought she might have been pregnant—I heard rumors, and she left town shortly after graduation, too—but I never wanted to believe that my son would run out on a girl if he'd gotten her pregnant."

"I can't believe Will would do that either." Meaning she didn't *want* to believe he was capable of that, but she didn't know him when he was eighteen. She didn't know why he'd left town and never returned, or why he and his uncle had quarreled to the point that Will had been disinherited. Or at least thought he'd been.

"It's a mystery." Maude sighed.

"Have you ever asked him?" Becky finished the drink and stood up. She would go back to her tomatoes and stop talking about Maude's son. She didn't want to know about Lily, she realized, feeling a little sick to her stomach.

"And let him think I believed the worst of him? No." Maude stood, too, and carried her glass to the counter. "Can I do something to help?"

"No. It's not going to take long to finish this next batch now that I have everything set up. You should go out on the porch, Maude, where it's cooler." Once again her stomach flipped, making her realize she shouldn't have eaten such a large lunch in this heat. "I'll join you as soon as Tommy wakes up."

"You work too hard," the older woman grumbled, but she refilled her glass and headed toward the porch, leaving Becky alone once again in the kitchen.

She wasn't in love with him, she thought. And even if she was, just a little bit, she would get over it. She didn't have any other choice.

"IT'S AWFUL HOT," Peter said, as they approached the creek. They were on their way home from what had become a very short ride. Will had realized pretty quick that it was just too damn hot to be out looking at cows and teaching a five-year-old kid how to stay on a horse.

"Yeah," he agreed, stopping by the water. "You want a drink?"

"Sure." The boy hopped off the horse like an experienced wrangler and led the horse to the water for a drink.

"We'll tie the horses in the shade," he told the boy. "We'll cool off for a minute before we head home."

"Neat!"

Will had no idea that that meant Pete would remove his boots and socks and stick his bare feet in the water up to his knees in a matter of three seconds. "Whoa, there, boy," he called. "That water is deeper than it—"

"I'm okay," the boy called, stepping farther into the muddy creek.

"Wait for me," Will hollered, stepping closer to the creek. He wouldn't mind taking off his clothes and jumping in that water.

"It's not cold," Peter said, moving forward.

"You've gone far enough." Will sat down and had one boot off when Peter slipped, fell over backward into the water and disappeared. Will was beside him in seconds, lifting the choking child into his arms with a silent plea that the boy was all right. He was choking, he was breathing, Will repeated to himself, depositing the boy on to the creek bank.

Peter coughed and turned wide eyes on Will. "That," he managed to spit out, "was pretty scary." Tears welled in his eyes.

"I'll bet." Will took a deep breath and willed his heart to stay in his chest. He'd thought he'd lost the boy there for a minute, and it had been scarier than riding any bull or half-loco bronc. He hugged the boy to his chest for a few minutes, and Pete rested his head on Will's shoulder.

"I don't know how to swim," the child confessed.

"The bottom of the creek is kind of uneven," Will explained. "You hit a low spot, that's all. But you should learn how to swim, even if you're just in a little creek."

"You gonna teach me?"

"Maybe." He set the boy on his feet and looked at him, soaking wet and muddy, too. "Your mother's going to have a fit."

"We have to tell her?"

"Yep. She's going to wonder why we're all wet." Becky was going to be upset when she learned he nearly let her son drown. He didn't relish explaining it to her, either. When the water had closed over Peter's head, Will had felt a panic like he'd never felt before. So this was what it was like, being a father. Trying like hell to keep the little rascals safe, swallowing the lump of fear after you knew that you couldn't do the job.

Peter wrapped his arms around Will's neck and gave him a hug. "I love you," the child said.

Will sighed and patted the boy's fragile back. "Yeah," he said, unable to say the words in return. He didn't love the child. He couldn't. He wasn't that kind of man. "Don't cry," he said, tucking the sobbing boy against his chest once again. "Everything's going to be fine. You're okay now."

"MY SON ALMOST drowned? How did this happen?"

Becky stood in the door to Will's bedroom as he stepped out of the bathroom. Fortunately for both of them, he thought, he was still wearing his jeans. He rubbed his wet hair with a towel and looked at her. "He fell in the creek," he replied. "I fished him out right away."

"You were supposed to be watching him."

"I was. He was a little too anxious to go in the water and didn't realize that the bottom dropped off. Those creek beds are—"

"I *know* how they are," she said, entering his bedroom. He backed up a few steps, hoping she'd come in even farther.

"Shut the door if you're going to yell," he said, wondering what those orange spots were on her shirt. She looked like she could use a shower, too. "I think Maude has company."

She shut the door, and Will tried to hide his smile. She was in his bedroom and she was marching toward him. She was talking to him, which she hadn't done in two weeks except to say things like, "Please pass the butter" and "Are you done with dinner?"

Becky looked upset, though, which was too bad. "Look," he tried, tossing the towel on the bed. "It was an accident. Nothing bad happened."

"It *could* have."

"But it didn't." He smiled down into those worried blue eyes. "It scared the living daylights out of me, too. I thought I'd never stop shaking." He put his hands on her shoulders. "He's fine, and I think he's learned to stop when someone tells him to stop. I'm sorry."

She tilted her head. "Really?"

"Really." He bent to kiss her lips. Just one of those reassuring kinds of kisses, of course. He didn't mean to slant his lips across hers. He certainly didn't mean for the kiss to lead to an overwhelming desire to make love to her.

"You're muddy," she whispered.

"You smell like... tomatoes." He nuzzled her neck. "Makes me think of making love to a pizza."

Becky pulled back. "Thanks a lot." She laughed in spite of herself. "I shouldn't yell at you. I'm sorry. You saved him, and that's all that matters."

He held on to her shoulders and spoke clearly, so that she wouldn't continue to worry over what might have happened. "The water wasn't deep. He lost his balance, that's all, though he gave me a scare there for a few seconds. Where is he now?"

"Oatey's giving him a bath. Suddenly he's too big for his mother to be in the bathroom with him."

He kissed her again. "I think you're just right," he said, taking her hand and leading her toward his bathroom. "And you could use a shower, too."

She looked down at her tomato-splattered shirt. "Thank you so much for pointing that out."

Will chuckled, leading her through the door. "I'll do anything, say anything, to get you to take a shower with me." He turned and started unbuttoning her blouse.

"You're limping again. You hurt yourself jumping into the creek, didn't you?"

He shrugged, opening her shirt and running his palms along her bare shoulders. "Nothing an ice pack won't cure."

She placed her hands on his bare chest. "Someone could find us in here."

"Not if we're quiet," he said, lowering his voice. "Oatey is taking care of the boys, Maude has company, and you and I are taking a shower."

"Together?"

He slipped the sleeves from her arms and tossed the shirt to the tiled floor. "Why not?"

"It seems so—" she hesitated, still touching his chest "—intimate."

Will resolved to be a hell of a lot more intimate than just standing under a shower head, but he kept his mouth shut and concentrated on unsnapping the waistband and opening the zipper of Becky's jeans. She wore cute little light blue bikini underwear, which he pushed down past her hips along with the jeans, and Becky wriggled out of them in quick fashion.

"Your turn," she said, standing naked before him. The snap had been undone earlier, since she'd interrupted him. She surprised him by reaching for him, sliding the zipper down with some difficulty. The denim was still damp and stuck to his skin. She eased soft fingers between his skin and his cotton briefs, and Will had to force himself not to take her right there on the bathroom floor.

She pushed his jeans lower, then lowered his wet briefs past his hips. He helped her then, knowing he couldn't take much more of her hands against his body. He kicked his clothes aside, then held her against him while he kissed her and took her mouth with his tongue. Her breasts were against him, a tantalizing feeling that threatened to take his breath away. They kissed for long moments, until he regained his senses. They wouldn't have much time, so he reached over and turned on the water.

"Wait," he said, reaching for her hair. He carefully drew the elastic from the end of the braid, then separated the thick strands of golden hair, running his fingers through the ripples made by the braid and draping the strands over her shoulders. It was as beautiful as he imagined, and he wanted to feel it on his skin when he made love to her.

He didn't know how they managed to shower without making love right then and there, in the cocoon of tile and steam. They washed each other with soap-slicked hands and watery kisses as the warm water rained down over their bodies. He turned off the water, grabbed at the towels stacked on a shelf, and led Becky toward his bed.

"We're soaking wet," she whispered, hesitating before the bed.

He wrapped her in a towel. "Better?"

She stood on tiptoe and kissed him. "Almost."

He lifted her by the waist and sat her on his bed, then proceeded to lick drops of water from her knees. She laughed, and he went higher, to the sweetness between her thighs. Sweet and ready and all his, Will discovered. He fished a condom from his nightstand, joined her on the bed, and entered her with slow, deep strokes.

Becky lay on her back beneath him, her legs drawn up to tangle with his, her eyes smiling as he moved within her. "I wish we had hours," he whispered. *Or a lifetime.* The thought surprised him, and he pushed it aside as he withdrew slightly, then moved into her again. He felt her climax almost immediately. She sighed and contracted around him, and he moved faster, deeper, until he'd come inside her with an almost alarming intensity. He rested his forehead on her shoulder until he could regain his senses, until his shuddering body could function enough to move from Becky's.

He rolled to his side and fell back on the pillow. His bare leg still touched hers, and he liked knowing all that wonderful female softness was beside him. At least for a few minutes. Becky turned to face him, so he tucked her into his arms and against his chest. The long hair was tangled between them, as erotic a feeling as he'd imagined.

"I should go," she said. "They'll be looking for me."

"I need you here."

She smiled as if he'd said something funny and attempted to move away. He lifted himself to release the yellow hair caught under his shoulder. He watched as she quickly found her clothes and dressed. She gathered her wet hair at the base of her neck, made a quick ponytail and looked back at him before she touched the doorknob. "I hope I can get back to the other end of the house without being seen."

"You look perfectly normal," he lied. She looked like a woman who had just been made love to. Her cheeks were flushed and her lips swollen from his kisses. She was barefoot, carrying her sneakers in one hand as she opened the door enough to peek out to the corridor. She didn't say goodbye, just slipped out of the room and shut the door behind her with a quiet click.

Will lay alone, naked and satisfied. He realized his knee ached, but the pain didn't register above the intense pleasure that still pulsed through his blood. He didn't know how he hadn't made love to her in two weeks, didn't know how they had managed to stay apart when it was obvious that any time they were alone, sparks flew and the temperature in their small part of Montana rose several degrees.

He had to leave, of course, though he'd missed most of the rodeo season and wouldn't be able to compete again, not seriously, until winter. If he didn't go soon, he wouldn't be able to. Becky would start expecting him to stay and be a respectable rancher. A father. A husband, even. He closed his eyes and wondered what the hell he was going to do. He'd enjoyed himself here. He hadn't expected to find a ready-made family in a place he hated.

Will sighed, willing himself not to think about the little blonde with the tempting body. He should have known better than to make love to Becky again, that's all.

BECKY WAITED four more days. Four agonizing days, waiting for relief from the worry that twisted her stomach and made her want to hide in her room with her head under the pillows. On Monday she could no longer stand the suspense and took the boys to town with her. They needed supplies, she told Maude. They would need more canning jars and lids, more sugar for canned fruit, more white vinegar for pickles. The pickling cukes had been hard to stay ahead of.

The smell of vinegar made her queasy, as did brewing coffee and cow manure. It was fortunate that Will spent his days acting like the foreman of this place, while she spent her time being busy in the kitchen. She'd begun to find the heat unbearable and the warm wind suffocating.

She'd found it hard to breathe normally, especially as the days crept slowly on. The trip to town didn't help. The boys were cranky, not pleased with the long ride in the station wagon. Tommy objected to riding in the shopping cart and Peter begged for expensive boxes of brand name cereal. She promised them ice-cream cones if they would behave for just a few more minutes. She paused for a long moment in the feminine products aisle, said a brief prayer and tossed a blue box into the cart.

"What's that?" Peter asked.

She wished he wasn't so darn smart. "Girl stuff," she said, covering the box with a large package of toilet paper.

"But it's blue."

"So?" Becky cleared her throat. "What kind of ice-cream cones are we going to get?"

That distracted them, thank goodness. She made it through dripping chocolate ice-cream cones, the hot trip home, Tommy messing his pants twenty miles from the ranch, and Peter's incessant questions about swimming lessons, having a friend spend the night, and when he could go riding again. She stopped on the side of the road and threw up. She told herself it was nerves. She wasn't used to this kind of heat—everyone said it was a record-breaking summer—or having an affair or canning this much fruit. She told herself it was too soon to feel sick, that it could be a touch of the flu. Or food poisoning.

Becky told herself a lot of things, until she locked herself in her bathroom later that afternoon, when the kids were resting and Maude had gone to visit yet another new friend, and the men were somewhere staying out of the sun. She followed the directions precisely, though her hands shook as she read them.

And when all was said and done, the results were positive. She had made love to Will Cody under the pine tree twenty-three days ago. She was ten days late and, according to the little plastic indicator, she was pregnant with Will Cody's child.

"LOOK ON THE bright side," Decker drawled. "He's still here."

Maude poured her old friend another finger of whiskey. "He's starting to talk about leaving again. Couldn't you come up with something else for him to fix?"

"Hell, Maudie, I broke that damn toilet twice. He'd start gettin' suspicious if something happened again." He took a sip of the drink and watched the sky darken from the kitchen window.

She sighed. "I'll make him promise to stay for the dance."

"Damn dance," Decker grumbled. "I suppose you expect us to get all spiffed up and lead them ladies around."

"Yes, I do. There will be other men there. I've sent invitations to all the ranches within seventy miles. You won't be alone."

He still didn't look happy. "Least it's a square dance."

"That was Theresa's idea. She said as long as we were going to have a barn dance, we might as well be authentic. She's such a smart woman."

"Authentic, huh? I think you've lost your mind. Camping trips are one thing, dances are something else."

"I've got three more trips lined up," Maude confided. "I put an ad in the Bozeman newspaper and got all sorts of phone calls."

He frowned. "Who's gonna do all the work?"

"We are. If my son is foolish enough to leave I suppose I might have to look around for a nice teenager to help us with the heavy things." She took another sip of her drink. "Maybe I should get someone to help Becky, too. She's looking a little tired lately."

"Peaked," Decker agreed. "Like she's got something on her mind."

"She's not happy. And you're right. She's not eating."

"Maybe she's sick. Oughta see a doctor."

Maude nodded. She didn't like the way the young woman picked at her food every meal. She seemed edgy, too, and never sat down and had a second cup of coffee in the mornings anymore. Maude missed those morning chats. "I'll suggest it. Do you think she's working too hard?"

Decker shrugged. "I thought Will was doin' most of the work around here, but what does an old cowboy know about women?" He answered his own question. "Not much."

Maude ignored him. She should have known better than to expect Decker to have any worthwhile insights. Something was wrong, although Will still looked at Becky with that certain expression, like he wished they were all alone. It was very romantic, and Maude was finding it harder and harder to ignore. Yet Becky was the problem. She acted cheerful, but not the kind of cheerful that a person could believe. It was forced, as if she was putting on a show for everyone. As if she didn't want anyone to know what was going on in her head.

Becky could be in love with Will, of course. And hurt that he was still talking about leaving. He'd put a few things in the bed of that old pickup truck, and he had made some phone calls and talked to some of his rodeo friends. He was still fixing things and teaching her how to keep track of expenses and keep up with the book-keeping. So there was still hope. As long as that young man was on this property, there was still hope. If ever two people were meant for each other, it was those two.

Maude hauled herself out of the kitchen chair and put her empty glass in the sink. "Well, I'd like to sit here and drink with you, but I've got to keep up with the books. Will's orders," she muttered. "Part of his new plan."

"Least you're fortified," Decker said, grinning.

"Take the bottle out to the bunkhouse," Maude said. "*Then* tell the men they're expected to dance with the ladies on Saturday night."

"Yes, ma'am," he said, standing up and taking the whiskey bottle by the neck. "That's one order I'd be happy to carry out."

"Thanks." Maude went into the office and sat down to survey this week's pile of receipts. Thirty minutes later, her pencil paused in midair and she squinted at the narrow piece of paper in her hand. She dropped her pencil, folded the piece of paper and carefully tucked it in the pocket of her jeans. Now it was time to get serious. It was time to come up with a plan, something that would make everything come out just right. Maude smiled, and patted her pocket. She'd been waiting for years for such a lovely, lovely gift.

"I THINK THIS is my dance," Will drawled, sweeping Becky in his arms as the band began playing "The Tennessee Waltz." She didn't have time to refuse, though she'd been staying away from him all week. There was no sense being around him, she'd decided. Not until she figured out what she was going to do about the baby.

The baby. She closed her eyes. Suddenly the inside of the barn was spinning around.

"Are you all right?" His arms tightened around her and she wanted to lean her head against his shoulder and scream, *"No, I'm not all right!"* Then he would demand to know what was wrong, and she would tell him that old condoms from first aid kits weren't reliable and she was going to have his child. And he would hold her very gently and tell her they would get married and live happily ever after. And pigs would fly and cows would milk themselves and the price of beef would triple.

"I'm fine," she said, and smiled. "Just a little dizzy."

"It's hot in here. I wouldn't have thought so many people would come to this shindig."

"Everyone brought food, and the band is playing for free."

"They should," Will said, trying to keep step with a band that wasn't quite on tempo.

Becky chuckled. "That's not nice."

He looked down into her face. "Where have you been all evening? I thought this would end without my getting to dance with you."

"I was, uh, busy. With the food."

"Too busy. Did the boys go to bed?"

"Yes. I hired one of the Carter girls to stay with them." The Carters were Dr. Theresa's nieces. There were three of them, all in high school and all sturdy, reliable girls who were happy to earn the money, Theresa had assured her. The middle one, Debbie, had come with her aunt and would stay until the party ended.

"My mother is in her glory," Will said.

"It was...nice of you to stay for her party. I know you must be anxious to be on your way."

"I couldn't refuse her." His arm tightened around her back again. "Becky, about this summer, I wanted you to know—"

"Don't," she said, stopping him from saying anything that would make her cry. "Let's not talk."

"But—"

"No. We had some wonderful moments together. You don't have to say anything. We're both adults who knew what we were doing." She looked up into his wonderful dark eyes and wondered if their baby would have those eyes. Those eyelashes. That mouth.

"If you keep looking at me like that, I'll have to scandalize the crowd and kiss you," he warned. "Maude would swoon with joy."

"And get her hopes up."

"Yeah." He stopped smiling and looked past her shoulder.

"What's the matter?" she asked, and turned around to see what he was looking at. A small group of people was gathered around someone on the dance floor. "Oh, no. It looks like someone fell."

Will dropped her hand as the music stopped and the two of them hurried to the edge of the straw-covered dance floor. Maude looked up at them and made a face.

"I slipped," she said. "I feel ridiculous."

Theresa was by her side, examining her friend's ankle. "Looks like a pretty bad sprain. Let's get some ice on it."

Becky tried to get closer to Maude, and Will was right behind her.

"I knew something like this was going to happen sooner or later," he muttered. He knelt beside his mother as Decker quickly produced a dish towel filled with ice from one of the washtubs that held cans of beer and soda pop.

"Let's get her to the hospital," Will said.

Theresa and Maude exchanged looks, then the doctor patted Will on the arm to reassure him. "Nothing's broken. I'm positive. But sometimes sprains are more painful and take longer to heal than breaks. She's going to need to stay off her feet for a while."

Maude shook her head. "Oh, dear," she said, sounding pitiful. Several people offered advice, Theresa kept the ice covering Maude's ankle and foot, and Maude insisted the band keep playing.

"How did you fall? Is there something slippery we should have cleaned up?" Will asked.

"I don't know," his mother said. "It just...happened."

He picked her up in his arms. "Let's get you to bed."

"I don't want to make a scene," she protested, but she put her arms around his neck and moaned a little.

Becky looked back at Theresa, who hurried after her patient. "Keep the ice on it," she said. "It will keep the swelling down."

Becky didn't know if she should follow them or act as hostess in Maude's place. She felt a little sick to her stomach again. Maude lying there hurt had been a frightening sight. Will looked furious, as if he wanted to burn down the barn.

Decker came up and stood beside her. "Don't worry, honey. Maude's fine. She's a tough old bird."

"He'll never let her stay now. Not if she's hurt."

Decker patted her on the shoulder. "I hate to think you're right, honey, but I'm afraid you jest might have a point."

12

"THAT'S IT," Will declared. He was clearly worried, and Becky didn't blame him for being upset. It had been a shock to see Maude helpless on the barn floor. Still, Maude hadn't looked as if she was in a lot of pain. Her cheeks had been flushed, and her eyes bright. Becky had decided her place was with the family.

"That's it," Will repeated, setting Maude on her bed. "You're coming with me. We're moving you to Billings, to a ground floor apartment within walking distance of—"

"I'm not going anywhere," his mother grumbled, arranging her skirts to protect her modesty. "Not with a hurt ankle. Right, Theresa?"

"Right," the doctor declared. She moved closer to the bed and made sure the ice pack covered Maude's ankle. "You're staying put, at least for a few more weeks."

"Weeks?" Will looked horrified.

The doctor nodded. "Weeks. At least. You'll have to leave now." She turned to Becky. "Would you help me get her into a nightgown and into bed, please?"

"Sure." The women waited for Will to leave the room, then Maude began unbuttoning her frilly white blouse. She smiled at Becky.

"I'm fine, dear. Don't worry about a thing."

"But—"

"Theresa and I can manage," Maude insisted. "Go out there and calm Will down. Tell him I'm not going anywhere."

"All right." Becky hesitated before turning the doorknob. "He's awfully upset, Maude. I think you should
start thinking about what he's saying, moving to Billings and all. You can't run the ranch with broken bones."

The old lady winked. "Worry about nothing."

Becky smiled as if she believed her, but once she left
the room and shut the door behind her, she leaned
against the wall and closed her eyes for a long moment.

"I knew something like this would happen."

She opened her eyes to see Will standing in front of her,
his hands crammed into his pockets, his dark eyes filled
with worry. "It was an accident," she said. "And she's
going to be fine."

"And what about next time? A fall from a horse?
Tripping on the stairs?" He shook his head. "I can't leave
her here. She's too damned independent. She thinks she's
invincible."

Becky didn't try to argue with him. It was obvious she
and the men couldn't keep Maude from harm. Their little balloon had burst: there would be no more pack trips
or barn dances; there would be no Paso-breeding business or day tours from the travel company Maude had
written to. It was over.

And that would save Becky from staying here and
growing bigger every week. It would save explanations
and her pride. Especially her pride. How could she tell
him she was expecting his child? Yet how could she not?

Theresa opened the door. "You can come in now." She
eyed Will. "Stop looking like she's dying. It's only a
sprained ankle, for heaven's sake."

He didn't smile, but let Becky step into the room ahead
of him.

"I'm calling that real estate agent first thing Monday
morning," he said. "I'll make all the arrangements for the
move to Billings."

"I'm not leaving," Maude said. "I can't go anywhere for at least a few weeks, right, Theresa?"

"Right."

Becky watched both women and wondered what on earth was going on. Maude looked remarkably cheerful for a woman who had just suffered a painful sprain and a scare, too. She looked almost happy to be in the bed giving orders. And Theresa, busy adjusting that enormous ice pack, was having trouble meeting Will's gaze. The two women were up to something, and Becky leaned against the far wall of the bedroom, folded her arms across her chest and watched to see what would happen next.

"Of course," Maude said, her voice suddenly weak. "You can go back to the rodeo, dear. We'll be fine here, just like we've always been."

"I can't leave now," he said.

"We'll talk on the phone, just like we always have," she assured him. Decker poked his head through the door.

"Just wanted to see how you was doing," he said, removing his hat. "Told the band I'd find out so they could make an announcement."

"It's a sprain," Theresa explained. "Nothing more serious." She looked at her watch. "I think the band stops playing at eleven. Will, why don't you go say good-night to the guests?"

"Good idea," Maude said, nodding. "It's only polite."

He scowled, but left the room. "I'll be right back," he said, and Decker followed him down the hall.

"There." Maude grinned at her friend. "I think that went very well, don't you?"

"Beautifully," Theresa said. "Though it's a good thing I've retired. I think I've stretched the Hippocratic oath far enough for one night, thank you very much."

Becky stepped forward, lifted the ice pack from Maude's ankle and saw a very normal-looking foot. Red from the cold, it wasn't swollen or bruised. She looked back at Maude. "You're not really hurt?"

"Nope."

"Maude! What are you doing?"

She shook her head. "I'm not telling you, not yet. We both have our secrets, don't we?"

Becky swallowed. Maude couldn't know. It was impossible. She'd carefully hidden the pregnancy-test box in the bottom of her closet until she could decide how to throw it away without anyone seeing it. Still, there was a light in the old woman's eyes that made Becky flush and back up a couple of steps. "You can't do this to him."

"He's going to stay," Maude declared. "All's fair in love and war."

"Not necessarily," Becky said.

"Oh, yes, it is." Maude smiled once again. "Don't worry, dear. Everything is going to be just fine. I have a plan."

"I should be terrified of your plans by now."

"Haven't they always worked out?"

Theresa hurried to adjust the ice pack as they heard footsteps in the hall. Several members of the Not Dead Yet Club stuck their heads in the door and wished Maude a speedy recovery. One offered to postpone Thursday's meeting until Maude was up and around.

"I'll keep you posted!" Maude waved cheerfully at the ladies in the doorway. Becky offered to make a pot of decaffeinated coffee and hurried to the kitchen. She didn't know exactly what Maude was up to, but she didn't want Will to think that she was part of his mother's scheme. Theresa and Maude would have to handle things by themselves.

And she would have to figure out what she was going to do with her own secrets.

THERESA DECLARED THAT SHE was going to take her niece and head home, Will paid the teenager before Becky could protest, and soon the house was quiet. Except for the sound of Maude arguing with him. Becky brought them coffee and tried to leave.

Will blocked her way. "Not so fast. Tell her you can't run this place by yourself."

Becky turned to Maude. "You know it's true, Maude. I'd be happy to try, but I think I'd better move on. I've been thinking about it for a while and, now that Peter is going to start school in a couple of years, maybe I should move back to Des Moines. I have an aunt there, and she'd be—"

"*You* are not going anywhere," Maude said, pointing to Becky before turning to her son. "And *you* are not selling this ranch. You can't now."

"Of course I can." He softened his voice. He knew she was going to have to make some big adjustments, and he was prepared to be patient. But he was also prepared to take care of her, even if she didn't want him to. "I know you love it here, but maybe we could lease it out, so we could visit once in—"

"No, you idiot, it's not your ranch anymore." She grinned. "You never met with that lawyer, did you?"

"Well, no, but—"

"And you never read your uncle's will, either."

Will frowned. "Why would I want to do that? It was over thirty pages long."

"You should have read it."

"Excuse me," Becky said, backing out of the room. "I'll leave you two alone to discuss—"

"This concerns you, Becky," Maude said. She nodded toward the pine chair by her bed. "Sit down, please."

Becky sat, but Will noticed that she didn't look too happy about it.

"Did Theresa give you any pain pills?" Will asked. "Are you feeling dizzy or a little woozy?"

"No. The will you didn't bother to read, son, states that the minute you have a child, the ranch belongs to him. Or her. Oh, you control running it and all that, but it's held in trust for your child. Or children. You can't sell it."

"So? I don't have any children. Never did."

Becky turned white when Maude looked at her, leaving Will wondering where all the air in the room had gone. Suddenly he found it hard to breathe. "What...are you talking about?"

His mother turned to Becky. "I'm right, aren't I?"

Becky opened her mouth but no sound came out, and she turned to Will with a helpless expression in those blue eyes.

"Becky?" Will stared at her, unwilling to believe that she could actually be . . . pregnant. The word gave him chills and, on a deeper, insane level, a feeling of pride. "Are you . . ."

She nodded and grew very pale. So pale, in fact, he was afraid she'd topple off the chair and crash to the floor.

"You can't sell now," Maude repeated, sounding quite pleased with herself. "It's out of your hands."

"That's quite a plan," he managed to say. He turned to Becky and steadied her with one hand on her shoulder. He looked down into those gorgeous eyes, but they didn't affect him. Not this time. "Were you going to tell me?"

She shook her head.

"I see," he said. "You were going to make a little visit to the lawyer first, I'll bet."

"No. I didn't know anything about the will," she said, turning to Maude. "You shouldn't have done this, Maude."

Will didn't let his mother respond. "Of course she should. She and her brother are more alike than I ever dreamed." He turned around and went to the door, then stopped. He was angry, his eyes cold as he looked at the women. "You've both got what you wanted now, what you wanted all along. The ranch is all yours to do with whatever you want." He looked at Becky again. "You took some pretty big chances, lady. Guess you thought it was worth it."

He slammed the door on the way out, and they heard his angry footsteps disappear down the stairs.

Becky pressed her palms together and willed herself not to tremble. "Maude, how could you?"

"No choice." Maude sat up and kicked the ice pack off her ankle. "I thought he'd stay if I was hurt. I didn't think the damn fool would start rattling on about selling out first thing Monday morning. I wanted him here, so you'd have time to tell him about the baby."

The baby. There was going to be another fatherless child on the Silver Valley ranch. The thought made her feel like crying, but she promised herself that she wouldn't cry in front of either Cody. "How did you know?"

"The receipt from the store. I record all the expenses now, the way Will taught me. Those new computer scanners tell what you bought, right there on the slip. I wasn't sure, so when I was in town yesterday I checked at the store and sure enough, that's what it was. One of those early pregnancy tests."

"You didn't know it was positive."

"Sure I did. You've been acting strange lately, my dear." Maude swung her legs over the bed and tried to take Becky's hand, but Becky pulled away. "Not drinking coffee, looking terribly pale and worried. I put two and two together and—"

"Came up with a disaster." Becky stood. "It was none of your business, Maude. You shouldn't have meddled."

"My future grandchild is none of my business? How can you say such a thing?"

Becky turned away and left the room without answering. She didn't follow Will downstairs. Instead, she walked toward the other wing, to her own room. She checked to see that the children were sleeping, then went into her room and locked the door behind her. She was going to cry for about a hundred hours and she didn't want to be interrupted.

"He's leaving." Maude hurried out of the kitchen and stood on the back porch to look out the window. "He's been packing up his truck since dawn."

"Well, Maude, what did you expect?" Becky fixed herself a cup of tea and wished the hot shower she'd taken had made her feel better. She'd finally drifted into sleep around two, then woke at six feeling queasy and weepy. But she'd be damned if she'd let either of them know it. "I'm going to be leaving, too."

"You can't," Maude said, still looking out the window. "Your child is going to own this place."

"I won't have Will thinking I tricked him into getting me pregnant just so I would get my hands on this ranch."

"He doesn't think that."

"Of course he does." Becky sighed. "Why wouldn't he?" She took another sip of tea and added more sugar. Tommy finished his cereal and patted his head with milk-soaked hands. "Don't do that, Tommy. Be a good boy."

"Okay," the child agreed, and dropped the empty cereal bowl on the floor and watched the plastic dish bounce twice and scare the dog. Lady, sensing that something was wrong, hid under the table while she waited for Peter to wake up. She whined as Becky retrieved the bowl and put it in the sink.

"Very nice, Tommy," Becky said, hoping this next child would be a girl. And then she felt like crying again, so she stuck her hands in the soapy water and started washing dishes.

Maude returned to the kitchen. "Your pregnancy was a lovely accident. I have to admit, it couldn't have worked out better."

"For you, maybe. I could have done it a little differently." She should have put that ad in the paper and found herself another job.

Maude patted her back. "It will all work out. My son won't turn his back on his child. He's just upset, but he'll come around soon enough."

"I don't know, Maude," Becky said, reaching for the frying pan. She breathed through her mouth so she wouldn't smell the bacon grease. "I'm not real happy about raising another child alone, but I don't want to hook up with a man who doesn't want me, either. I had one bad marriage, I don't want another one."

Maude looked as if she wanted to argue, but Peter came down the back stairs and yawned. "Hi," he said to everyone, then disappeared under the kitchen table to greet the dog.

Decker walked in, his face solemn. "That boy's in a real bad mood this morning. He's loading up his truck right now. What the hell's going on around here?"

"Hell!" Tommy grinned at the cowboy. "Hell!"

"Now you be quiet," the old man told him. "No sense sitting in that high chair cussing like an old wrangler."

He looked at Becky. "You don't look too good either. You and Will have a fight?"

"I guess you could say that."

"Well, go make up. This place is crazy enough as it is." Decker poured himself a cup of coffee. "That boy said he's figuring to enter the rodeo in Casper tonight and ride tomorrow. What kind of talk is that?" the man grumbled.

Becky knew she should talk to Will privately. She'd considered that last night, in the quiet of her room, after she'd used thirty or forty tissues and her eyes were swollen almost shut. She'd realized then, through buckets of tears, that she loved Will Cody and wanted to have his child. But she didn't want him to marry her out of pity or for a chunk of Montana real estate or for some noble reason about giving the child a father.

She wanted him to love her, and stay because he loved her. She wasn't going to settle for less. She didn't need him. She could manage quite well on her own, which she had spent the last two and a half years proving to herself and anyone else who happened to notice. If Will Cody wanted to leave, he should leave. She wasn't going to do a damn thing to stop him, either.

NO ONE STOPPED him. Will packed his few belongings in the meager light of dawn and loaded the truck bed with the few things he'd brought with him last month. He didn't pause to question why he was so angry, but it seemed to well out of him as if it had been there for a long time waiting to boil over.

The cowboys stayed out of his way. Men had a hell of a lot more sense than women, that was certain.

He was going to be a father. The words hummed along with him as he worked to clean out the horse trailer and get the little mare ready for a trip. *He was going to be a father*. How crazy was that? He wasn't a father, though. He was a goddamn sperm bank, and those energetic sperm had handed the deed to the SV into the hands of Becky's waiting egg.

An accident of nature or the result of brilliant planning? Maude had seen that they were alone on the mountain, Becky had been warm and willing, there were condoms in the first aid kit. Condoms that were old, that could have had pinholes put in them and been resealed. He'd heard of those things happening. He just never thought it could happen to him.

But a child meant keeping the ranch. And Becky and Maude had been hell-bent on keeping the ranch. He looked back toward the house. If only Becky would come out and talk to him, tell him it wasn't true, look up at him with those soft blue eyes and tell him it had all been an accident, that she had never pretended to love him....

He shook his head. She wasn't going to come out and say that, because none of it was true. The only truth was that he loved her, loved her as he had never loved any woman before, and she was content to let him go.

She had what she wanted, and what she wanted wasn't Will Cody.

LADY STUCK HER HEAD through the narrow window that separated the cab of the truck from the covered back. Once again she whined, a high piercing sound that went right through his head.

"All right," he told her, and pulled off to the side of the road. "You're the one who wanted to ride in the back." He shut off the ignition and got out of the truck. They'd been on the road for almost an hour, heading south on a back road toward Wyoming, and there wasn't another car or truck in sight. He hopped out of the truck and lifted the back window. And froze.

"Hi, Will," the child said. Peter was curled up on Will's sleeping bag, his head using the saddle as a pillow.

"What the hell," Will began, then took a deep breath. He didn't want to scare the child, but the temptation to holler at him was irresistible. He took a deep breath as Lady came over and licked his face. "What in God's name are you doing in the back of my truck?"

"Going with you and Lady," the child replied, as if it was a sensible explanation.

"Going with me and Lady," Will repeated, pushing the dog from his face. "What do you think your mother's going to say about this?"

The child shrugged. "She won't be mad. 'Cuz I'm with you."

"I think you're a little wrong there, kid." There had been no goodbyes. Of course, he waited for Maude to come out and scold him. He wondered if Becky would follow him to the truck and tell him he was going to be a father, the way a man should hear it. She hadn't. He'd said goodbye to the men, then returned to his truck. "How did you get in here?"

"I just did, that's all."

Which was why the dog had uncharacteristically insisted on riding in the back, of course. Will held out his hand. "Well, come on. It's not safe for you to ride back here. Come on up front."

Peter untangled himself from the sleeping bag and crawled over to Will. "Okay. Are we going to a rodeo? Decker said you were gonna ride in one again."

"No." He lifted the boy from the truck and set him on the gravel road. Lady hopped out, too, did her business in the grass, then trotted back to them with her tail wagging. "We're going to head back to the ranch, before your mother has a fit."

Will settled the boy in a seat belt, shoved Lady between them, and turned the truck in the opposite direction. So much for leaving. He couldn't get away from the goddamn place no matter how hard he tried.

He turned the radio on and began to whistle.

"DON'T SEE HIM nowhere around the barns," Malone declared. "I think he's with Decker. Must be."

"No." Becky shook her head. "Decker thought he was with you."

"Then mebbee he's with Oatey."

"Oatey's asleep in his bunk. Last night wore him out."

"Ain't surprised," the man muttered. "He danced with all those women, every dance." He patted Becky's arm. "Now, don't you worry. Pete's probably taken them action figures and is building a fort somewhere under a tree where we can't see him. I'll keep lookin'."

"All right. Thanks." Becky held Tommy in her arms and made another search of the house. She called Peter's name until Tommy held his chubby hands over his ears and cried for her to stop.

"Pete go for ride," the child whimpered.

"A ride? I don't think so, honey." She set Tommy down and got on her hands and knees to peer under Peter's bed. "Peter McGregor, you had better not be playing a trick on me!"

Silence. And the knot in her stomach tripled in size.

"Daddy's 'ruck." Tommy sat down and started to sob. "Me, too. I want go Daddy's 'ruck, too."

"Daddy's truck?" She turned to him. "Did Peter go in Daddy's truck?"

Tommy cried harder, so Becky scooped him up into her arms and went to find Maude. Peter had been upset

that Lady was leaving, furious that Will was packing up
to go away. Becky had thought he'd gone off to cry, so
she'd given him time to be alone. But when she'd looked
for him she hadn't found him in any of the usual places
around the outbuildings, and the cowboys hadn't seen
him either. That was almost two hours ago, which meant
that Will, unaware he had an extra passenger, could be
close to Wyoming by now.

Becky, with Tommy in hand, caught up to the woman
in the garden. "I think he's gone with Will."

The older woman turned pale. "Will wouldn't take the
child, I know—"

"No, of course not," Becky hurried to reassure her.
"But Peter was so upset. He could have climbed into the
truck with the dog. Do you think I should call the state
police? Will could be in Casper before he discovers him."

Maude looked past her and smiled. "I think he already has. Look."

HE DIDN'T HESITATE this time when he approached the
long road to the ranch. In fact, his foot bore down on the
accelerator as much as he dared. There was no knot in
the pit of his stomach, no feeling that he'd rather be anywhere else on the earth except here, heading toward the
Silver Valley ranch.

No, this time he felt like he was coming home. There
was a kid beside him, and a woman waiting for him.
There was a baby who called him Daddy and one on the
way, a boy or girl who should know who his or her father was. He'd had a lot of time to think, this long hour
back to his home. There was no fooling himself any
longer. He was glad to be turning around, relieved to
have a reason.

Will sped as fast as he could, letting the dust fly behind him in thick gray clouds. He didn't have a chance

to park the truck in his usual spot. The women met him partway down the road, and he stopped right there and rolled down his window. "I've got him," he said, unnecessarily, because Peter sat in the front seat waving to everyone like he was in a damn parade. Becky opened the passenger side and was hugging and scolding the child at the same time. She looked at Will.

"Thank you," she said, her eyes suspiciously bright.

"I would have come back anyway," he replied, wishing he could take her in his arms and tell her exactly what was in his heart. But she had her arms full, and Tommy peeked around her knees and grinned at him. Will opened the door and stepped out in time to see his mother hurrying to greet him.

She wasn't limping. "You've recovered," he said, trying not to laugh.

"And so have you, I think," was her reply. She gathered up the boys and took them by the hand. "I'll keep these two out of mischief while you figure out what's right in front of your face," she told her son. Lady barked, so Will opened the back gate and let her out.

Then he and Becky were alone, standing in front of the dusty truck. Several of the men, pretending to be fixing something, stood by the fence and sneaked peeks at them from underneath the brims of their hats.

"Maude will be watching from the porch," Becky said.

He didn't want to talk about Maude. "Marry me."

"Because I'm having a baby? No, thank you." She lifted her chin. "I'm raising two kids alone now. I can raise one more."

Will stepped closer and took her by the shoulders. "I came back to do the right thing."

She raised her eyebrows and didn't look impressed. "You've never wanted this ranch. You made that clear. So why did you come back? Because of the will?"

For you, he wanted to say. "My uncle had the last laugh. Or so he thought. He kicked me out of here sixteen years ago because he thought I'd gotten my girlfriend pregnant. He wanted me to pay her off. He didn't want to share one acre of the ranch with a stranger."

Becky went pale. "Lily?"

He nodded. "Yep. Trouble was, I was still a virgin and Lily had been two-timing me with an older guy. When he left town, she decided to tell people the baby was mine. She had her eye on this ranch and my uncle's money."

"And your uncle didn't believe you."

"He was more than happy to think the worst. We had a fight, I left. He told me not to come back, that I was a spineless, irresponsible coward." He smiled down at Becky. "And, from the way I acted this morning, he was right. It was just when I heard that part about the will, I knew that old bastard was still trying to run my life, and I resented the hell out of it."

"I didn't mean to get pregnant," she whispered.

"And I didn't mean to fall in love with you, either," he said, gathering her closer into his arms. "So tell me you'll give me another chance and you'll make an honest man out of a broken-down rodeo rider."

She pulled back to gaze into his face. "Are you sure? You're the last man in Montana I thought would be ready to settle down and become a father."

"And a husband," he added, touching her lips with his. "Don't forget the most important part."

Becky, wanting to believe, kissed him back. But when they drew apart, she still hesitated. "I don't want you marrying me because you think you have to. For the baby."

"Sweetheart," he said, gazing down at her with a tenderness that made her knees go weak. "There is no other place I'd rather be."

"Really?" She wanted to believe, wanted to hold him close to her forever, wanted to have his children and sleep in his bed each night and know that when she woke in the morning he would be there. Forever.

"Really." He tucked her hand in his and headed toward the house. "Do you think you have time in your busy schedule to arrange a wedding?"

Becky smiled. "I'll bet Maude and the Not Dead Yet Club will be happy to help. Any objections to getting married on the ranch?"

"Honey," he drawled, smiling from ear to ear. "If you want this cowboy, you can have me anywhere, anytime."

"I like the way you think," she said, stopping to let him kiss her one more time before they entered the house. From somewhere in the distance she heard Maude and the cowboys cheer.

* * *

The next two BACHELORS & BOOTIES books from Kristine Rolofson are October and November Temptations®. Look for *The Only Man in Wyoming* and *The Next Man in Texas*.

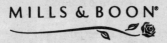

FREE!

FOUR FREE
specially selected
Temptation® novels
PLUS a FREE Mystery Gift
when you return this page...

Return this coupon and we'll send you 4 Temptation novels and a mystery gift absolutely FREE! We'll even pay the postage and packing for you.

We're making you this offer to introduce you to the benefits of the Reader Service™– FREE home delivery of brand-new Temptation novels, at least a month before they are available in the shops, FREE gifts and a monthly Newsletter packed with information, competitions, author profiles and lots more...

Accepting these FREE books and gift places you under no obligation to buy, you may cancel at any time, even after receiving just your free shipment. Simply complete the coupon below and send it to:

MILLS & BOON READER SERVICE, FREEPOST, CROYDON, SURREY, CR9 3WZ.

READERS IN EIRE PLEASE SEND COUPON TO PO BOX 4546, DUBLIN 24

NO STAMP NEEDED

Yes, please send me 4 free Temptation novels and a mystery gift. I understand that unless you hear from me, I will receive 4 superb new titles every month for just £2.20* each, postage and packing free. I am under no obligation to purchase any books and I may cancel or suspend my subscription at any time, and the free books and gift will be mine to keep in any case.
(I am over 18 years of age)

T7YE

Ms/Mrs/Miss/Mr _____
BLOCK CAPS PLEASE

Address_____

_____

_____ Postcode _____

This month's
irresistible novels from

THE HEARTBREAK KID by Alison Kent

Tyler Barnes had a healthy masculine ego, not to mention a heartbreaking grin and an incredible body. But Sophie North was only passing through and she'd sworn never to live her life at the mercy of her own passionate nature. But Sophie should have known, nature *always* gets its own way...

THE LAST MAN IN MONTANA by Kristine Rolofson

Bachelors & Booties

Will Cody returned to his ranch to sell his inheritance. Family life, staying in any one place for too long just isn't for him—until he meets the new 'foreman', Becky McGregor. She's gorgeous, sexy and a *mother*! She's determined he should keep the ranch...

THE ALL-AMERICAN MALE by Glenda Sanders

Cassaundra Snow was thrilled when she met Chuck Granger, but as powerful as her response to him was, she dreaded the moment when his reporter's instincts would tell him that she was living out a fairy tale. And that her story was Cinderella *in reverse*...

SEX, LIES AND LEPRECHAUNS by Renee Roszel

Devlin Rafferty was as handsome as the devil, but Laura Todd was a woman with a mission—to find the heir to a fortune—so she couldn't afford to be distracted while she was in Ireland. But maybe a pleasurable little diversion would be all right. Except it became more than a diversion and it was a bit *too* pleasurable...

Spoil yourself next month
with these four novels from

Temptation ®

THE ONLY MAN IN WYOMING by Kristine Rolofson

Bachelors & Booties

Dell Jones proved his worth when he rescued Allison Reynolds
and her twin baby girls. But even though he was successful,
dependable and loyal, he didn't believe that the woman with the
face of an angel and the body made for sin would settle for a man
like him...

SOME KIND OF HERO by Sandy Steen

Mail Order Men

Jared Markham didn't want love, but he did want companionship.
Shannon Kramer was more than he'd expected, but she was going
to be a lot more trouble, too. On the run from her ex, Shannon
needed a hero, not a husband. And Jared found himself
desperately wanting to be both.

THE GREAT CHILLI CAPER by Lorna Michaels

Wade Phillips was an old-fashioned private investigator, one
who didn't want a woman on his heels wanting to be his partner
and getting into trouble! But if he wanted the Brewster case—
which he did!—then he had to have Samantha Brewster, too.
Sam was a great-looking woman; what a shame she wanted to
be Jane Bond!

AMBUSHED by JoAnn Ross

Men of Whiskey River

Clint Garvey had decided the way to avoid heartbreak was to
avoid people. But Sunny was determined to change his attitude,
to fix his life and to find him true love. She seemed to think she
was his fairy godmother! Clint should have sent her packing, but
he felt like begging her to stay.

Meet
A PERFECT FAMILY

Shocking revelations and heartache lie just beneath the surface of their charmed lives.

The Crightons are a family in conflict. Long-held resentments and jealousies are reawakened when three generations gather for a special celebration.

One revelation leads to another - a secret war-time liaison, a carefully concealed embezzlement scam, the illicit seduction of another's wife. The façade begins to crack, revealing a family far from perfect, underneath.

"Women everywhere will find pieces of themselves in Jordan's characters"
—Publishers Weekly

The coupon is valid only in the UK and Eire against purchases made in retail outlets and not in conjunction with any Reader Service or other offer.

- -

50P OFF
COUPON
VALID UNTIL: 31.12.1997

PENNY JORDAN'S *A PERFECT FAMILY*

9 904170 210508

0472 00195